FICTION

LUCID
Bill Kelly 3

THE ODDS ARE GOOD
Josh Pachter 22

BONE SOUP
Michael Bracken 25

SUICIDE INSURANCE
Gerard J Waggett 42

THE POWER OF THE DOG
Leone Ciporin 51

A GRAVE MISTAKE
Rachel Amphlett 63

ONLY THE DESPERATE COME HERE
Michael Mallory 67

A LITTLE HOUSECLEANING
David Bart 76

A NUMBERS GAME
A You-Solve-It by Bruce Harris 84

INQUIRIES & ADVERTISING

Address: Suite 22, 509 Commissioners Road West, London, Ontario, N6J 1Y5

Advertising: Email info@mysteryweekly.com

Editor: Kerry Carter **Publisher:** Chuck Carter **Cover Artist:** Robin Grenville-Evans

Submissions: https://mysteryweekly.com/submit.asp

LUCID

Bill Kelly

"That's the funny thing about Alzheimer's."

"Funny?"

"Well, not *funny*." A look of horror crossed Lucy Pritchard's face the moment the word came out of her mouth, and Ted couldn't help but be struck by her piercing blue eyes.

They were kind eyes. Caring eyes. She was a sensitive girl, and it was clear she felt badly at even the suggestion that she found humor in the plight of the afflicted. "I mean, it's just awful. It's terrible. To lose yourself like that. Lose who you are." Lucy frowned, emphasizing her point. "That's part of why it's been the focus of my studies. If I can make a difference, even with one person, you know?"

Ted *did* know. He remembered his own long-ago idealism, how he had cruised out of grad school with the same hopefulness, only to crash a few years later into the multi-car pile-up that was life's realities. Still, Ted wasn't interested in crushing other people's ambitions. Maybe she could make a difference. He certainly wasn't here to stop her.

"So what's the funny thing about Alzheimer's?"

"I'm sorry." Lucy apologized all over again. "Maybe *ironic* would be a better word?"

"Works for me," Ted said, attempting a breezy smile, wondering if she could detect the physical strain required for him to produce it.

"The ironic thing," Lucy explained, her voice taking on the helplessly preening authority of the over-educated, "is that memories are lost in reverse order. A person's more recent memories are far more fleeting than the ones from their earlier years. You see, Alzheimer's disease begins in the hippocampus—" She paused, self-conscious. "Do you already know all this? I don't want to bore you."

Ted shook his head to indicate that he did not.

It was a lie of course.

He was already well-versed about the hippocampus, the region of the brain responsible for translating experiences into memory. He knew from overseeing a floor full of empty, vacant faces that when Alzheimer's gets to work on the hippocampus, recent experiences never have the chance to become memories. But when one is surrounded day-in and day-out by the old, addled and drooling, you are in no hurry to send away pretty young women with soft skin and long blonde hair who show up in your office wanting to discuss their possible graduate work. So the forty-five-year-old director of the Westwood Senior Center let the twenty-eight-year-old grad student explain the hippocampus in all its wonder, enjoying the view as she spoke.

"You see, it's not until much later that the disease affects the regions in the brain where older memories are stored, so those memories are available even into the later stages of the disease." It was the unearthing of these older, lingering memories, Lucy explained, that formed the basis of her proposed therapy. "To help both the patients and the caretakers learn new communication skills. That way, hopefully, their conversations can be a source of comfort, instead of both sides just ending up frustrated with each other."

Ted made a cursory show of making a decision, though he'd already resolved to grant Lucy Pritchard permission to do whatever she desired—midnight wheelchair races down the corridors if she wanted—anything if it meant she'd return here tomorrow.

"Well it's certainly worth a try, if you want to give it a shot. How would you like to proceed?"

"I guess I'd need to meet the appropriate patients," Lucy said, considering her answer, "the ones who are affected, I mean."

"Sad to say we have no shortage of candidates." Ted smiled warmly at her and she smiled back. All too politely, he thought, much to his disappointment. "Obviously some more severe than others."

"Lucy Pritchard, this is Carl Volchoff. Lucy's going to be doing some volunteer work with us, Carl."

It was the following afternoon and Ted Troutman stood between Lucy and Carl, making the introductions. A longtime resident of the facility in the waning stages of his disease, eighty-two-year-old Carl sat slumped over in a green plastic-cushioned chair in the TV room, his head lolling as he stared into space.

"Hello, Carl." Lucy leaned down, shaking the old man's gnarled spotted hand. Though she spoke in the loud, measured tones that typified initial contact with the elderly, her voice was warm, friendly. "What did you do before you came here, Carl?"

But Carl didn't answer. He just continued to stare. After a long moment, Ted spoke up on Carl's behalf, as if they were two guys out at the bar and Ted was the designated wingman for his overly shy drinking buddy.

"Carl was a mechanic in his younger days. He worked at a shop specializing in foreign models. Spitfires and MGs, Jaguars. Isn't that right, Carl? All those flashy sexy models I can't afford on my salary."

Lucy smiled charitably at Ted's weak joke.

Carl kept on staring.

Ted and Lucy toured the facility, and Ted introduced her to the rest of their twelve officially diagnosed Alzheimer's residents. Lucy was patient and gracious with each of them, making a point of opening their shades to let the light in and counteract the sundowning effect. Just as with Carl, she asked questions to gauge their level of engagement, pointing to their cherished curios and family portraits, inquiring exactly who was who. At each visit, Lucy would set down a small portable audio recorder, innocuously taping her conversations with the patients for later analysis.

"Have you settled on anyone in particular?"

Ted and Lucy were sitting in the break room afterward, and Ted felt himself hoping that none of his staff would stop in to grab coffee or eat their lunch. He wanted Lucy all to himself.

"I think I'm leaning toward Carl."

"Carl?" The choice surprised Ted. "Really?"

"You don't think he's a good candidate?"

"No, I was just thinking, given how far along he is in his Alzheimer's, well, he's probably in the worst state of anyone here. Seems like he'd be a real challenge."

"I think that's what draws me to him. How else will I know if these techniques are really working?"

"I would just hate to see you end up, you know, discouraged."

And stop coming here, Ted said to himself. Please don't choose Carl.

"Oh, I don't get discouraged." Lucy said with a modest certainty.

"Well then." Ted somehow couldn't conceive of disagreeing with her. "Carl it is."

Ted wasn't supposed to share the resident's records. They were strictly confidential. But Lucy was so good about it. She didn't really 'ask' after all. She only mentioned, in a strictly off-handed manner, that it would be *so* helpful if she could read them.

Besides, she smelled so good. Ted wondered about her brand of perfume. Or was it one of those body sprays? The kind that women applied right out of the shower—

"Carl played piano?"

"Did he?" Ted looked up, caught off guard by Lucy's question.

They were sitting in his office eating lunch, Carl's file spread out between them. Ted had unlocked the file cabinet and pulled it out, sliding the file across the desk to Lucy. He contemplated accompanying this gift with a conspiratorial wink, but he knew he was a terrible winker, and he worried that it would create a corny, avuncular impression that would only serve to heighten their age difference.

"According to what his daughter wrote down, it was a hobby of his." Lucy was eating her food truck taco as she studied the information sheet that the residents— usually the resident's closest relative—filled out at admission. "Auto repair, old movies and boogie woogie piano."

"Really?" Ted watched as Lucy absently looped her long blonde hair around her fingers. It occurred to him that he could die happily if he knew the afterlife consisted of watching Lucy play with her hair.

"Sometimes engaging in an activity that was once familiar to a person can awaken sense memories." Lucy looked up at him. "Do you have a piano here?"

"Well yes. An old upright in the rec room, but ..."

"Perfect. We could start there."

With the help of the orderlies, Lucy lifted Carl from his wheelchair and set him down on the piano bench. Lifting the cover, she brought his calloused old mechanic's hands up to the keyboard, resting them like curled talons on the black keys.

"Why don't you play us a tune, Carl?" Lucy encouraged. "Any old favorite that suits your fancy?"

Carl sat quietly, his head resting against his chest. Reaching out, Lucy gently brushed his limp hands along the keyboard, giving the impression that they were merely stumps and not fingers capable of individual articulation. The keys made a harsh, discordant sound. After a moment, Lucy returned Carl's hands to his lap.

"Maybe we can try again later?" Lucy's smile was unwavering. Ted was impressed. She didn't sound remotely discouraged.

And she wasn't.

The next morning, Lucy showed up even earlier.

She had found the photo album in the bottom drawer of Carl's bureau; a bit of an invasion of Carl's privacy, Ted thought. Then again, Carl would never know and

Ted was not about to mention it. He was too busy trying to think of an excuse to ask Lucy out to dinner.

"You say the daughter doesn't come by anymore?" Lucy whispered to Ted as the both of them sat in Carl's room with him. The orderly assigned to care for Carl, Isabella, a middle-age Mexican woman in peach-colored scrubs, watched the proceedings from the doorway, making no effort to conceal her skepticism.

"She died a few years ago. Cancer," Ted softly explained, though he suspected he could scream the news through a bullhorn and Carl would be none the wiser.

Moving her jean-clad legs forward so that they were touching Carl's bony pajama covered knees, Lucy opened the album up between them with the pictures facing Carl.

"Well now, Carl. Tell me. Who's this handsome fellow?"

The image Lucy pointed to was an old black and white photo taken on the deck of an air craft carrier. A grinning young sailor stood with a monkey wrench in his hand. Shirtless and tanned with muscular arms, he sported powerful shoulders and a large navy tattoo across his chest. Ted's eyes went from the photo to Carl. That same tattoo, a faded blue anchor with "U.S. Navy" curled around it, could still be seen beneath the strands of white chest hairs peeking through Carl's pajama top.

Age is a real son-of-a-bitch, Ted thought as he inspected Carl's sunken frame, not wanting to think about what ravages time would exact on his far less impressive body.

"1952. USS Essex." Lucy read the caption scrawled beneath the photo. "Is that the ship you were stationed on, Carl?"

Carl stared at the photo, saying nothing.

"I see you have a wrench here. Were you a mechanic? Is that where you first learned to work on engines?"

And still, Carl did not speak. Not a peep.

Having witnessed as much of this fruitless exchange as she could bear, Isabella spoke up in a thick accent.

"Honey, I have an ashtray at home that talks more than he does."

"Isabella. Please," Ted chastised. Rather than acknowledge this dressing down, Isabella turned from the doorway and walked away.

"I thought that went pretty well."

Ted knew he was lying, but felt conflicted. Walking with Lucy away from Carl's room, he was torn between the urge to be completely candid with her and the even stronger desire to mouth whatever bromide he thought might comfort her.

"That's sweet of you, Ted. But we both know that was a disaster."

"I guess it was." Ted said, eagerly contradicting himself. "I hope you're not thinking of giving up?"

"Not a chance. But the photo album did give me an idea."

"Oh yeah?"

"Well, it's not always the case, but sometimes …" Lucy hesitated, biting her bottom lip. Ted imagined it was him biting it. "Memories can be jogged by sensory experiences."

"What's your idea?"

"It's definitely unconventional." Lucy looked in his eyes. "And I'd need your help."

Ted smiled involuntarily.

She needed him.

Lucy stood at the curb outside the facility next to Isabella, Carl in his wheelchair between them. It was an unseasonably warm November day, and the ugly red scarf wrapped around Carl's slumping head probably wasn't necessary.

"I think you might like this surprise, Carl," Lucy said, to no reaction.

Isabella refused to join Lucy in her display of forced enthusiasm. Like most of the employees, she depended on the predictability of her daily routine to manage her heavy work load, and this young coed's bullshit experiment—rolling this potted plant of a man outside for a field trip—was an unwelcome disruption. Still, she said nothing. She knew her boss liked this pretty white girl. There was no point in making waves.

"He should be along any minute now—" Lucy started to say.

That's when they heard the roar of the engine.

Lucy and Isabella turned their heads, following the sound to the end of the block as a white 1964 Karmann Ghia convertible tore around the corner.

Carl's head remained slumped.

"Hey, kids," Ted shouted with a forced jauntiness as he pulled the stylish little car to a halting stop at the curb beside them. "Who's up for a spin?"

Ted reveled in Lucy's smile of pleasure, telling himself it was intended for him as the two women loaded Carl into the passenger seat. Once they had buckled the old man into place, Lucy deftly hopped into the small back seat. Glancing back, Ted's eyes couldn't help but be drawn to the deep V in her V-neck sweater.

Pulling the car away from the curb, Ted threw the car into second gear, thrilling to the feel of Lucy's hair accidentally brushing against his neck as she leaned in to speak to him.

"This is so great, Ted. Who lent you the car?"

"A friend of mine owed me a favor." Ted yelled over the engine, enjoying this image of himself as a roguish speed demon instead of a staid retirement home administrator. "A doctor I know. I send a lot of patients his way."

It would have been a perfect ride, Ted thought, were it not for the presence of their special guest. Ted would have much preferred Lucy sitting beside him instead of Carl, perhaps grabbing his arm to steady herself in those moments when he took the curves with daredevil abandon.

"Enjoying the ride, Carl?" Lucy asked, sadly reminding Ted that he was not the sole focus of her interest. "Did you like driving in these cars as much as fixing them?"

But even as the engine purred, the wind blowing through everyone's hair like a Vogue fashion shoot, Carl's face remained impassive, saying nothing.

Keeping one eye on the road, Ted caught a glimpse of Lucy's expression in the rear view mirror. Her brow was furrowed in discouragement. Ted didn't care for this look. It made her appear less attractive. He wanted to make that look go away.

"At least we're enjoying a nice day out," Ted said, smiling with a forced bravado that only managed to make Lucy look more forlorn. Born with bad instincts that never got better, Ted made the mistake of trying harder. "I mean that's *something* at least—"

They were all startled by a loud booming sound, the car suddenly lurching as Ted felt the engine lose power. Their forward progress immediately slowed to a crawl, forcing Ted to steer the car toward the curb. Grinding his way through the gears, Ted finally came to a dead stop as Lucy leaned forward from the back seat.

"What's wrong? What happened?"

"I'm not sure, I—"

"What was that noise?"

"I think the engine misfired."

"But *why* did it misfire?"

"I don't know." Ted's voice faded as his mechanical incompetence was laid bare, his true identity exposed. He was not a rakish Steve McQueen-esque speed demon after all, but merely an impotent pencil pusher. Ted had no clue as to why they'd suddenly gone from eighty-five miles an hour to being stuck on the side of the road, motionless.

An unexpected voice provided the answer.

"Carbon on the plugs."

Lucy and Ted turned to Carl at the same time, both startled by the soft croaking words coming out of the old man's mouth. "Gotta rev her up," Carl continued. "Blow out the carbon."

Ted thought that Lucy's smile of surprise appeared almost beatific.

It was only later that he understood why.

The "carbon on the plugs moment" as Lucy referred to it thereafter, heralded an unprecedented breakthrough. Suddenly Carl Volchoff, the man for whom everyone thought speech was lost forever, couldn't stop talking.

"That was Mike Scully. We were on the Essex together. Crazy guy. We were on shore leave in Singapore. The son of a bitch ran up a hell of a bill in a whorehouse. I had to give up three months' pay to cover his ass, and we were still short. We barely got out of there alive."

Ted and Lucy were in Carl's room again. Lucy had flipped the photo album to the next page: a black and white photo of young Carl with his arm around another sailor, a curly haired bruiser with massive shoulders. Staring out from the land of long ago, their grinning faces beamed with youthful energy and mischief.

"I was in a jam 'cause I sent money home to my ma." Carl explained, describing the moment from sixty years ago as if it was last week. "Fortunately, I was pretty good at craps. Won it all back by the time we docked in Hong Kong."

Carl smiled at the memory. Lucy and Ted smiled back even as they struggled to imagine this old man as a young one, sailing around the world, winning crap games, and running for his life to escape the perils of exotic foreign whorehouses.

"Jesus, Carl. That's enough! Lay off him."

Carl could hear Scully yelling at him, pleading for him to stop bashing his fists into the face of the fat Asian bouncer, and even though a small voice inside his head told him that Scully was right—he *was* going too far—Carl couldn't help himself.

"Christ, Carl. You're going to kill him." Carl felt Scully's baseball mitt hands on his shoulders, yanking him, still swinging, off the now unconscious bouncer.

"I'm not through with him yet, you fuck," Carl yelled at his best friend.

Pulling his massive arm back, Scully smashed his fist into Carl's jaw.

Carl felt the world go black around him.

When next he opened his eyes, Carl looked around to see he was lying in a dark room. He was reclined in some sort of strange hospital bed, though the heavy wooden bureau and night stand looked familiar. A harsh fluorescent light peeked in from the crack beneath the doorway.

Though he had no mirror to confirm his suspicions, Carl sensed that he was very old now. He could feel an aching weariness deep in his bones.

Where the hell had all the years gone? How had he ended up here?

Hopefully Scully would show up and bail him out of this place.

After that whorehouse fiasco in Singapore, that Irish bastard owed him.

The next morning found Lucy sitting across from Carl again. Standing beside her, Ted watched as Lucy flipped the album open, holding up another photo for Carl's review.

"June and me. Our wedding night. Vegas. '57." Carl squinted at the photo: a black and white snapshot of an old-school steak house, all dark wood paneling and red leather booths. A circle of handsome men in sharply cut suits and glamorous women in cocktail dresses flanked the young bride and groom as they carved a small white cake, everyone smoking and drinking and having a grand old time.

"Nice. Looks very romantic," Ted observed.

He meant it too. It *did* look romantic, and if his comment happened to give Lucy any ideas, well, all the better. He was a single guy after all, no kids. A homeowner with plenty of disposable income, Ted could swing a weekend getaway to Vegas no problem.

"That's sweet," Lucy said. Studying Carl's intensely curious expression, she turned the page to reveal—

Carl in a school auditorium, standing behind a nine-year-old girl wearing a Brownie uniform and holding up a cadette badge—a father and daughter milestone.

The man who'd so viciously brutalized the whorehouse bouncer had his arms wrapped gently around the girl. She was looking up at him, smiling, her whole world contained within her gaze.

"Gracie," Carl said softly, and started to weep. The tears rolled down his cheeks, his mind still lost in that long-lost moment. Grabbing a tissue, Lucy reached out and dabbed at Carl's tears in a tender display of compassion.

"You're probably tired, Carl." Ted fought the catch in his voice, both touched and embarrassed by this display of naked emotion.

"I guess I am," Carl said. "A little."

Ted had waited until the last possible moment to ask her, the two of them saying nothing as they walked down the hallway from Carl's room to his office, both of them still caught up in their journey into Carl's past.

Ted knew he had to do it soon or risk losing his nerve completely. Lucy had pulled on her black wool coat and scarf, turning on her high cork heels to leave when Ted finally managed the question.

"Hey, Lucy. I wondered if you wanted to have dinner?"

"Dinner?" Lucy turned back to him. "Oh, Ted. To be honest, I'm awfully tired."

"That's okay. Forget I asked," Ted said, attempting a land speed record for self-effacement.

"Oh, no. I'd really like that," Lucy reassured. "Maybe we could do it another time? you know ... after?"

"After?"

"After this is all over. When I'm finished with my project. I just really want to stay focused."

"Of course." Ted smiled, pleased. She'd said 'yes' after all. True, it was at some indeterminate later date, which may or may not ever come to pass.

But it was a yes nonetheless.

"Come on, Daddy. Play the boogie-woogie."

Carl was sitting in the living room of the little row house that he'd managed to purchase through the VA and was still struggling to make payments on.

Somewhere in the back of his mind, Carl knew that he'd lose this house. Though he couldn't remember exactly *how* he knew these things, he understood that at some point down the road he'd end up divorced and living alone in a shitty apartment. He also knew that his little girl would grow up unhappy, that it would be his fault—that she would die of cancer.

But Gracie was alive, at least for now. She was sitting on the polished pine floors, looking up from her homework with an expression of pure adoration, as if she saw something in him that he couldn't see in himself. Something good and kind and decent.

Lifting his calloused fingers onto the keys of the Baldwin spinet, Carl started to play.

Isabella heard it first.

She was eating lunch at her station, watching one of the afternoon talk shows on the small TV set. A couple of fools were talking about knocking up young girls and using a lot of nasty language, when suddenly their voices were drowned out by the sound of piano playing.

It was an old-timey kind of music, coming from the rec room, sloppy and loud and thumping.

Curious, Isabella dropped her homemade tamale back into her Tupperware dish and made her way down the hallway, the music growing louder as she turned the corner.

She was greeted by the sight of Carl in his wheelchair hunched over the piano, his old arthritic fingers banging out a shaky but determined road house boogie woogie.

Seated around the room, the other residents grinned with pleasure as they listened, bobbing their heads to the beat. Some of them were even clapping.

"I'll be damned." Isabella said, laughing over the rattle of Carl's plunking piano.

Arriving a moment later, Ted stood beside Isabella, equally astonished by this spectacle.

And then he turned to hurry back to his office.

He needed to call Lucy.

"Who is this woman, Carl?" Lucy asked.

Carl looked at the picture, and though Ted could see he clearly recognized her, he seemed confused by her photo. Carl leaned in closer, squinting.

The picture looked like it was taken in the 80s, a high school class photo perhaps. A pretty young woman with curly brown hair and an easy, approachable smile, she wore a red collared sweater and oversized tortoise shell glasses.

"Do you remember her, Carl?" Ted repeated Lucy's question. "Do you remember her name?"

Carl hesitated, his voice resistant even as he answered. "Deidra."

"Is there anything you can tell us about her?" Lucy asked.

Carl paused again. This one lasted twice as long.

"She's dead."

So's everyone else in this goddamn album, Ted thought to himself. His next thought was that he was grateful Lucy couldn't read minds.

"Maybe there's a story about Deidra you'd like to tell us?" Lucy had used this segue before, a jumping off point for Carl's reminiscences.

Carl's eyes never moved from the young woman's face as he answered.

"I killed her."

Ted stared at the old man, stunned. "Carl?"

Lucy inhaled softly.

And Carl started to talk.

"Volchoff. Punch out."

Carl looked up from under the Jaguar's hood. "I'm almost done," he answered. Christ that little prick Monahan didn't know when to let up.

Monahan stuck his head out the office door. "You're headed into overtime. Finish tomorrow morning."

Carl was reluctant to stop working, but he didn't have a choice. God knows he was in no hurry. He would have worked all night if they'd paid him. Hell, maybe if they hadn't. All that was waiting for him at home was that empty apartment; maybe a quick phone call to Gracie if that bitch ex of his would let him talk to her.

Carl had no hobbies, no outside interests, and with nothing else to do, he knew that he would invariably head out to the bars. Carl was also conscious that this wasn't a smart idea. He'd been drinking way too much lately.

Still, less than two hours later, his fate was sealed.

Cleaning up at the shop, he had rubbed goop all the way up to his forearms to get the car grease off. Eating McDonald's in his car, he drove home and took a shower.

He didn't shower alone of course.

He was joined by a fifth of Crown Royal.

Already thoroughly lubricated by the time he arrived at The Last Call, Carl noticed a new girl working the bar. She was pretty. Brunette with big glasses and a nice shape.

Deidra.

She looked a little young, but that was okay with Carl. He kept trying to talk to her, but she was giving him the brush-off, telling him she was busy, though hell, she seemed to have enough time to talk to all the other guys in the place.

Try as he might to make a good impression, Carl could tell that she was becoming increasingly annoyed with him. That strained smile she gave him when he flirted with her, the way she started washing glasses when he tried to tell her a joke. Granted, his jokes were off color, hell, downright dirty, but this was a bar after all, not a church social. When the bouncer finally kicked him out just before closing, Carl was pissed.

Walking to his car, Carl thought about driving home. He decided to wait for Deidra instead.

When Deidra finally locked the front door and made her way across the gravel parking lot, Carl stepped out of shadows to speak with her.

She looked up at him, startled. "What do you want?" she asked.

"I just wanna talk to you." Carl slurred.

"I don't want to talk. Just leave me alone."

And then she started walking toward her car. Hurrying actually, like she couldn't get away from him fast enough. Like he was some sort of creep.

That made Carl angry. Who was she to judge his intentions? It reminded him of the way his ex treated him, the reason they had all those fights, the reason she'd filed that restraining order. Jesus, everyone always thinking the worst of him.

Christ, all he wanted to do was talk to her.

"Just leave me alone," Deidra shouted as he followed after her. "I just want to go home."

Carl wasn't exactly sure what happened next. The liquor complicated things. He had downed so many shots he couldn't be sure. When Deidra turned and ran back toward the bar, it set something off inside him. Carl knew he had to stop her, to let her know—*let the world know*—that he wasn't the goddamn animal everyone made him out to be.

Running after her, Carl grabbed at her arm, or was it her shoulder—*her neck?*—and she ended up hitting her head against the concrete. Had he been helping lift her up off the cement or, God help him, had he been pounding her head against it?

Carl's memory on this point remained cloudy, both on that night and for years after.

At any rate she had stopped breathing.

It wasn't his fault, but Carl knew he'd be blamed anyway.

He had to find some place to put her.

It couldn't be the woods off to the side of the parking lot. That would be the first place they'd look.

Carl remembered the auto salvage yard the shop used. They had 55-gallon drums there, hundreds of them. He knew just the spot. A patch of dead land where they dumped the oil. No one would look for her there.

Wrapping the girl's body in the plastic tarp he used to lay out parts when he did repairs at the apartment, Carl placed her in his trunk. Taking a sip of flat soda from his earlier McDonalds run, he did his best to sober up.

Cruising down Highway 19, Carl drove like a nun, praying like one that he wouldn't be stopped.

It was only when he hit the freeway that Carl noticed his own blood was running down the front of his shirt. Deidra had managed to stab him in the neck with her keys. He couldn't risk being found wearing this.

Carl made a mental note to bury his shirt as well.

Looking around the room, Carl remembered that he was old now.

He was in the room again, with the young woman and the middle-age man, whoever they were.

Carl had never told anyone the story about the girl before. He had long ago locked it up in a box and thrown the box into a dark black hole deep inside him. Taking the box out again, opening it, telling the story, made him feel lighter, a weight lifted.

"Even after all these years," Carl said at the end of his story, "I can still hear her screams."

"Oh my god," Ted said, quietly mortified.

"Would you like a glass of water, Carl?" Lucy said with surprising calm.

She poured a glass from the plastic pitcher on Carl's beside table and handed it to him. "You must be thirsty after all that."

Carl took the glass and drank, grateful.

"You okay?" Lucy asked.

It was past 11pm. Lucy and Ted stood by their cars in the near empty parking lot. Carl had fallen asleep in front of them and they had walked outside together, both still too shocked to speak.

"I'm not sure." Ted was winding and unwinding his car keys in his fingers. "His story? It couldn't be true, could it?'

"Why wouldn't it be?" Lucy asked. "What does he gain by fabricating that story? Is he even capable of making up something like that at this point?"

Ted knew that logically she was right.

"What are we going to do about this, Ted?"

Ted didn't want to think about it. "Honestly, I don't know. I have no idea."

"You want to go out? Get something to eat?"

Ted was surprised by Lucy's question. This wasn't how he'd hoped things would evolve between them. "I'm not really hungry. Not after that."

"I'm not hungry either." Lucy took a nervous breath. "It's just that after that story, I don't want to be alone."

They drove in Ted's Lexus.

The light from the instrument panel cast a soft glow on Lucy's face as she stared out her window, lost in thought.

"Look, if you want, we could just go somewhere and have coffee. Hang out at my place. Or yours?" Ted knew he sounded like he was trying to take advantage of the situation, and he scrambled to regain the high ground. "I mean, what would you like to do?"

Lucy slowly turned and faced him. "I want to go there. I want to go to the spot."

Ted told himself she hadn't said this, that maybe he'd misheard her?

"I don't understand. What spot?"

"You *know* what spot, Ted. You heard him. We both did."

"Lucy—"

"Do you think we can just *ignore* it?" Lucy looked in his eyes and Ted realized she was seething with anger, an unbridled indignance in search of a target. "Just leave that poor woman out there. Like *he* did?"

"Why would we go there, Lucy. I mean, for what purpose?" Ted knew he sounded defensive, but he couldn't help himself. "What would we do there?"

"You live in a house, don't you?" Lucy's tone was sharp and condescending. It caught Ted off guard. "I mean you're constantly prattling on and on about how you own your home, bragging about your low fixed mortgage, how you're too smart to get stuck with an adjustable rate."

Ted caught a glimpse of a Lucy he'd never seen before. There was a sting in her words, an underlying impatience; the suggestion that perhaps all this time she'd merely been tolerating him, that maybe she even found him a little irritating.

"Yes, I have a house," Ted said, confused. What point was she trying to make?

"Okay." Lucy softened her tone. "So you have a backyard I'm guessing? Garden tools?"

"Well, yes. But I still don't understand what this has to do with—"

"You own a shovel, don't you?"

Ted could only nod. He finally understood.

The signs on the auto yard's fence read "Security Patrol" and "Guard Dog on Duty," but the rusted chain link and the stillness of the high weeds suggested a Mars-like absence of life. A single buzzing fluorescent light shined over the entrance sign, leaving the rest of the perimeter draped in darkness.

Guided by the powerful mag flashlights Ted kept in his trunk, Ted found a section of fence that had come loose from its posts. Using a shovel to push it aside, Ted followed Lucy into the yard.

Carefully making their way through the high rows of hulking old vehicles toward the back of the salvage yard, they saw the rows of rusted old 55-gallon drums, just as Carl had described them. Ted moved his mag light in an arc across the barrels, both of them spotting simultaneously—

A round patch of grassless dead earth, soaked through with dried motor oil.

Ted's shovel hit something twenty minutes later. The jarring metallic sound was followed by a small gasp as Ted looked up to see Lucy's troubled reaction. Lucy shined the flashlight down as Ted fell to his knees, chopping at the rusted metal with the shovel until finally a chunk of it fell off completely.

Kneeling down beside Ted, Lucy pointed the flashlight into the blackness of the drum.

The beam of the Maglight caught a flash of a clear plastic tarp, and beneath it, the unmistakable outline of a woman's gym shoe.

"So what do you want to do now?"

They were back in Ted's car. Completely freaked out, Ted was trying to hide the distinctly unmasculine panic in his voice.

"We have to go to the police of course," Lucy said with a contrasting calmness. There was that hint of impatience with him again.

"The police?" Ted didn't need to think long to find problems with that idea. "And say what? We're trespassing here."

"We don't have to tell them we were here. We'll just tip them off. Tell them where to go."

"Based on what? How will we explain knowing there's a goddamn corpse here?"

"We have to play them the tape of his confession. So they know he did it."

"You recorded his story?" Ted sounded surprised, even as he suddenly remembered the small digital recorder she'd used in all her patient interviews "to document her project."

"He's an old man. It's just a story. That doesn't prove that he actually did it."

"What about his DNA? The shirt? His blood?"

"You'd need a sample of his DNA. Even if the cops had reasonable suspicion, that would take a court order. For us to get involved in all that, Lucy, the facility—"

"We don't need a court order."

Lucy produced the glass she had handed to Carl out of her purse. The one he drank from. She'd had the foresight to place it in a Ziploc bag.

Things moved quickly after that.

The murdered woman, full name Deidra Peterson, had gone missing twenty-five years earlier. The detectives working the case had always suspected Carl Volchoff. A single mother and part-time bartender, Deidra had been seen arguing with Carl at The Last Call on the night of her disappearance. His alibi, that he'd gone home directly after the bar, was shaky at best. And there were those unexplained cuts on Carl's neck, which his boss, contrary to Carl's story, did not believe were work related.

Carl had said nothing at the original trial, and the jury, absent a body or any direct physical evidence, was left with little choice but to acquit.

Now cold case detectives, working from Lucy's recorded confession, were able to 'locate' Deidra Peterson's body. Carl's bloody shirt was indeed inside the plastic tarp, and with the help of modern science, police were able to match the killer's blood to the DNA on Carl's water glass. While making no effort to argue the physical evidence, Carl's court-appointed attorney pointed out that his client, in the later stages of Alzheimer's, was unfit for trial, and requested a dismissal based on incapacity.

The dismissal was granted.

Later that night, at home, Ted watched the news. In a brief segment on the case, old video footage from the original trial was shown. A much younger Carl sat at the defense table staring forward without emotion.

Ted continued watching as the camera panned to the victim's family. A distraught older woman, Deidra's mother, Alice, held a pretty young girl on her lap, Deidra's daughter. No more than three years-old, the little girl had long blonde hair and piercing blue eyes.

She was absently looping her hair in her fingers.

"You knew it was him? The entire time?"

Ted was standing in the doorway of Lucy's efficiency apartment. Her eyes went out to the hallway, as if afraid they might be overheard.

"Do you want to come in?"

Ted followed Lucy inside as she walked to her kitchenette and refilled her wine glass.

"Would you like something to drink?"

"I'd like you to answer me." Ted adopted the wounded expression of a man owed an explanation.

"What do you want to know? Did I know it was him?" If Ted was expecting some sort of contrite mea culpa, an unrepentant Lucy had no intention of obliging him.

"Yes, I've known it was him my entire life."

"The photo of the woman in his album? Your mother? Deidra? How'd it get in there?"

"I put it there," Lucy said without shame. "After he had his breakthrough with the piano, all the other stories. Once I was fairly certain he'd remember her."

"You used me, Lucy." Ted was starting to realize the scope of her deception.

"No, Ted. I used him," Lucy practically spit the words out. "His illness. I used it against him. I used it for justice for my mother."

"My god." Ted looked at her, not quite recognizing her anymore. "Was any of this genuine? Do you even care about people with Alzheimer's?"

"I care about murderers with Alzheimer's." Lucy's voice was somehow even colder, and Ted felt unnerved.

"Well," Ted said, weakening. "I guess you got him."

"No, I didn't. He got away with it. He wasn't even punished."

"The judge said his disease was punishment enough."

"Not for me." Lucy took another large sip of wine, her fists clenched, her voice trembling with anger. "The idea that I actually helped him? Gave him back his memory? That I helped provide that bastard even a moment's pleasure in his twisted dotage."

"I don't think they're happy memories." Ted was trying to be helpful. "He seems, very ... I don't know ... tortured."

"*He's* tortured? What about my mother?" Ted immediately regretted his words as Lucy shook her head, incensed. "The fact that he gets to stay right where he is, comfortable and taken care of, that ... fuck. I swear to God if I had five minutes alone with him."

"You can't go back, Lucy. For your own sake." Ted saw the crazed look in her eyes and it scared him. "The facility has a restraining order against you. You'd be arrested. As it is, I barely kept my job after all this. I mean shit, the publicity, we've lost six residents already. Families worried that we're housing a murderer, which I guess we are."

"I don't care if they arrest me," Lucy said.

"I care," Ted said, suddenly said without intending to.

"Thank you, Ted. I know you do." Lucy forced a calming breath. "And I appreciate it." Reaching out, she took his hand. Ted realized it was the first real physical contact they'd shared.

"Listen ... Lucy." Ted struggled to find the words, to tell her everything he'd felt for her since the moment she first walked into his office.

Instead, Lucy said them for him.

"You like me, Ted? Don't you?"

Ted could only manage a small nod.

Ted knew that it went beyond merely liking Lucy. He knew that he had developed a deep affection for her, that he probably loved her. He sensed just as strongly that his feelings were not reciprocated, that she didn't love him back, that it was entirely possible that she felt nothing for him at all.

Ted didn't care.

Ted held the pillow down tight.

Carl's muffled screams managed to find their way up through the cheap hospital foam and polyester pillow case. Fighting his last great battle not in a far-off foreign entanglement, but on an orthopedic hospital bed in Kansas, Carl struggled mightily against Ted's efforts. Despite his unimpressive middle-age body, Ted pressed his entire weight, all thirty surplus pounds, against Carl's pillow.

After a few last gasping lurches, Carl finally went limp.

Sitting at her station, Isabella saw Ted exiting Carl's room a few minutes later, noting to herself that she'd never seen Ted enter a resident's room at night. Still, she wasn't about to say anything. She had a son in college. He was going to be a paramedic, maybe even save some lives. No point in making waves.

Ted intentionally showed up late the following morning, after Carl's body was discovered. Ted's doctor friend, the one who lent him the car, signed Carl's death certificate. A common enough occurrence at the facility, it was more or less a formality. No one requests autopsies for eighty-three-year old men with Alzheimer's.

Driving by Lucy's place after work, Ted found her front door ajar, her apartment empty except for a few cardboard boxes. According to the manager, she had left no forwarding address.

Driving home, Ted parked his Lexus in the double garage where his garden tools still lay strewn on the floor from his night out with Lucy, the night they had dug up her dead mother.

Taking a shower, Ted climbed into bed and absently turned on the news.

He wasn't alone. He was joined by a fifth of scotch.

Waking in the middle of the night, Ted found himself gasping, short of breath, his eyes wet. He realized he'd been crying.

He could still hear Carl's screams. 🖎

THE ODDS ARE GOOD

Josh Pachter

It was six-thirty when Sherilyn Crabbe and Ginny Krause walked into the Bamboo Room—Haines, Alaska's one and only tiki bar, around the corner from the Hammer Museum—so there were still plenty of seats at the bar.

"Where's this husband of yours?" Ginny asked. "Isn't he supposed to meet us here?"

"He'll be along," Sherilyn said. They slid onto chromium and red plastic stools and hung their purses on hooks screwed beneath the bar.

Christy, who had taken over the establishment when her parents retired, materialized in front of them. "What'll it be, ladies?"

"Sign says the halibut and chips is famous," Ginny smiled. "I guess I'll—"

"Let's hold off on food till Barney gets here," Sherilyn cut in. "We'll just have a drink for now, Chris."

"Dalton Trail?"

"You know it."

"And you, Sherilyn's friend? What can I do you for?"

Ginny studied the list taped to the mirror behind the bar. "What's the Black Fang like?"

Christy pushed out her lower lip and shook her head. "I'd work my way up to that one, if I was you. It's pretty heavy, eight-point-two percent ABV. The Spruce Tip Ale is awesome, but it won't be on tap for another two weeks."

"Have you got an amber?"

"Try the Eldred Rock. Caramel malt, Cascade hops, five percent, goes down smooth as silk."

"Is it local?"

"Yes, ma'am, made right here in town, about a three-minute walk from where you're sitting."

"All right," Ginny decided. "I'll go with that."

Christy pulled their pints and spun two coasters onto the bar.

Ginny cautiously tasted her beer, her blonde curls haloing her expertly made-up face. She patted her mouth with a paper napkin. "That's nice," she sighed.

Sherilyn threw an arm around her friend's shoulder and hugged her. "God, it's good to see you, Gin! Now, spill it: what are you *doing* up here in the ass end of nowhere?"

"Well," Ginny said, "you remember Roger?"

"*Roger*? I thought you got rid of that creep five years ago."

"Four. Then I married Jerry on the rebound, like fifteen minutes after the divorce was final. I wish you hadn't moved up here to the Last Frontier, Sher—you would have talked me out of it."

Sherilyn nodded knowingly. She was a brunette, her hair short and layered, her big brown eyes attractive without mascara or shadow. "Another loser?"

"Major. Be glad you never had the pleasure. I can't *wait* to meet your hubby."

Sherilyn glanced at her watch. "He must've got held up at work. He'll be here." She took another small sip. "So, are you avoiding my question, girlfriend? Why did you drag yourself all the way up to the Land of the Midnight Sun?"

"I'm *lonely*, Sher," Ginny said plaintively, "and every man I meet in Wisconsin is either a workaholic or unemployed. You keep writing me the odds are good up here—"

"Fifty-two percent male," Sherilyn beamed proudly, "highest male-to-female ratio in the US of A."

"—so I thought why not play the odds? I quit my job and sold my car, and here I am. I figure *somebody* in the Frozen North must need a good bookkeeper. I've got some savings, so I'll rent myself a little apartment and—"

"Not right away, you won't. We have a finished basement we don't use, you can park yourself there for a while, check Haines out and see if you like it. If you do, well, *then* you can think about an apart—"

A burly man in a lumberjack shirt and a bushy black beard beneath a sparse head of hair beginning to go gray slid onto the stool next to Ginny and pressed his shoulder up against hers. "Hey, there, missy," he rumbled, "I heard you say you're looking for a man."

Ginny recoiled from the unwelcome contact. "A *man*," she said, "not a reject from a Monty Python sketch."

Sherilyn put a hand on her friend's arm. "Gin," she said, "you don't—"

At that moment, a skinny guy in ripped jeans and a filthy Alice in Chains T-shirt crackled through the front door, a ski mask pulled over his face, a stubby Charter Arms Undercover .38 Special in his hand.

"Money," he shouted, the gun trembling spastically. "Now!"

"Oh, Jason," the lumberjack growled, "you think we don't recognize your voice? Take off that stupid mask and put the gun away and have a beer. I'm buying."

"I'm *serious,*" the kid insisted. "I want all the cash from the—"

The lumberjack reached out and lazily swatted the gun from the boy's hand. He pulled a pair of cuffs from behind his back and, ten seconds later, had the kid flat on his face on the Bamboo Room's wooden floor.

"Ow," the kid wailed. "These things *hurt.* Can you loosen them up a bit, Barney?"

"Barney?" Ginny said.

"I tried to tell you," Sherilyn grinned. "Barn, this is my old friend Ginny, up from the Lower Forty-Eight. Ginny, this is my husband."

"But he—"

"Oh, don't mind Barney, he's got a weird sense of humor."

"Sorry if I offended you," the lumberjack said. "I was just kidding around. Skootch over, hon."

Sherilyn moved down a stool, and Barney squeezed in between them. Christy set a glass of what looked like tar in front of him, and he took a long swallow, his boot resting lightly on Jason's back. He chugged half the pint of Imperial stout and thumped down the glass. "Black Fang," he said, wiping the back of his hand across his mouth. "Thanks, Chris."

He turned to Ginny. "So you *did* come north looking for a man, is that right?"

Ginny drained her first Alaskan beer. "Sher tells me the odds are good," she said.

"The odds *are* good," Sherilynn repeated, slapping the back of her husband's head tenderly. "But I'll tell you what we say up here in God's country, girlfriend: the *goods* are odd."

BONE SOUP

Michael Bracken

Sheriff Sherri Fine stood inside the Chicken Junction High School gymnasium, arms folded beneath her breasts, and listened with growing revulsion as Senate candidate Clayton Holms railed against the godless heathens of the opposing party. Two of her deputies, both off duty, were in the audience paying rapt attention. Two others with similar political leanings were cruising the county.

Her radio crackled. "Sheriff?"

She thumbed her radio. "Go ahead."

"You need to see this," said Deputy Carl Smith. "We got us a dead body."

The Senate candidate no longer held Fine's attention. As she headed for the door, she asked, "Where you at?"

"Devil's Canyon Creek Road. Twelve miles west of the highway."

"On my way."

In the entire history of Arroyo County, no one from her party, let alone a woman, had ever served as sheriff. No one expected Sherri Fine to be elected, not even the local party loyalists who had put her name on the ballot. When her multi-term predecessor had died of a heart attack on election eve, it was too late for his party to replace him, so his supporters sat out the election while hers did not. Fine bested the dead man by a single vote.

Born and raised in Waco, Fine moved to Chicken Junction, Texas, following graduation from McLennan Community College with a paralegal/associate of applied science degree, earned in her late twenties after too many years spent behind the counters of various fast food joints. Her entire law enforcement experience prior to swearing in as sheriff consisted of a single year working in the Arroyo County district attorney's office, and the deputies in her department—all but one of whom had voted for the dead candidate—did not take kindly to her assumption of the late sheriff's duties.

The one deputy who hadn't supported the dead man was waiting for Fine when she arrived at a derelict pole barn a mile up a dirt road that intersected with Devil's Canyon Creek Road twelve miles west of the highway. The road once served as the private drive for the long-abandoned Latham Ranch. She parked her department-issued SUV next to Deputy Smith's, not far from a pickup truck long past its prime. As she climbed out, Smith approached and greeted her by touching the brim of his Stetson with the tip of his finger.

"Sheriff."

She nodded once in acknowledgement. "What do you have, Carl?"

"J.P. over there"—he cocked a thumb toward a weathered octogenarian standing off to the side—"was picking for treasure and found a body instead."

"Show me."

Deputy Smith led the sheriff into the barn where she took one look at the scattered bones and said, "That ain't a body."

"Was once."

"You touch anything?"

"No, ma'am."

She glanced out of the barn toward the old man. "What about him?"

"Says he didn't. Once he recognized the bones for what they were, J.P. called Maybelle and she sent me to take a look-see."

"What was he doing out here?"

"Picking."

She waited in silence until Deputy Smith explained.

"Pickers like him rummage through abandoned buildings, looking for anything they can sell for profit—old denim, jewelry, bottles, metal signs, and the like. Half the stuff in the new antiques shop in Quarryville came out of places like this. City people eat this crap up."

"Take J.P.'s statement, get his contact information and send him on his way," Fine told her deputy as she unclipped her iPhone. "I'll see if I can find us a CSI."

The Arroyo County Sheriff's Department lacked the funds for a dedicated crime scene unit. On the rare occasion when a situation involved death, the department relied on assistance from Chicken Junction's police department. Within minutes, she had an investigator assigned to her and she used her smartphone to photograph the skeletal remains *in situ* while awaiting the investigator's arrival.

By the time Sheriff Fine stopped for a late dinner at the Bluebonnet Grille, two topics dominated local gossip—that afternoon's political rally at the high school and the discovery of skeletal remains at the long-abandoned Latham Ranch. She ordered chicken-fried steak and mashed potatoes in white gravy from Deputy Smith's teenaged daughter Madison, and then nursed a tall glass of sweet tea while waiting for her meal to arrive.

Gossip swirled around her.

"Probably some Mex headed north."

"Can't build a wall tall enough to keep them people out."

"Hell, they already got most of the jobs over at the meat processing plant."

"Clayton said he'd put a stop to that."

"Clayton Holms? You're on a first-name basis with the man?"

"I ought to be. He signed my yearbook."

"That was twenty-nine years ago, Betty Sue."

"I still remember it like it was yesterday."

Madison arrived with the sheriff's dinner. As the teenager placed the warm plate on the table, she pointed to the unopened textbook at Fine's elbow and said, "My daddy says you're almost finished with your classes."

"Almost." Halfway through her four-year term, Fine had only eight hours of training remaining before she met state requirements for commissioned peace officers. "What about you?" she asked. "You given any thought to what you're doing after graduation?"

"Baylor," Madison said. "I want to go to Baylor, but Daddy says it's too expensive."

"You know I'm from Waco, don't you?"

"Yes, ma'am."

"I have a friend who works in financial aid," Fine said. "If you're still interested in Baylor when you're a senior, let me know and I'll introduce you."

"Thank you, ma'am," Madison said. "My daddy said you had a good heart. I appreciate it."

The teenager stepped away when another diner signaled, leaving the sheriff to her meal. She wasn't alone long.

Carter Bledsoe straddled the chair opposite her. "What's this I keep hearing about a dead body?"

"Bones," she told the Arroyo County district attorney, her boss when she worked as a paralegal. "Some hair we think may be the deceased's."

"And you didn't think to call me?"

"There's no evidence of a crime."

"What's your gut telling you, Sherri?"

"That I'm hungry," the sheriff said. "I haven't eaten since breakfast."

Bledsoe glanced at Fine's chicken fried steak and mashed potatoes drowning in white gravy. "You keep eating like that and you won't just have Sheriff Danville's job, you'll have his figure and his heart condition, too."

"I'm glad you're watching out for me, Carter." She forked a piece of chicken fried steak into her mouth. "As soon as I learn something that might interest you, I'll give you a shout."

Several days later, she did. With the autopsy report on her computer screen and her desk phone pressed against her ear, Sheriff Fine said, "The victim's a young woman, mid-teens, been dead near-on thirty years. The proximate cause of death is a fracture in the back of her skull."

The DA asked, "Was she murdered?"

"Looks that way."

"Any idea who she is?"

"Jolene Delacroix," Fine told Bledsoe. "She was reported missing and the file is still open."

"Your first cold case."

Defensively, Fine said, "So how many have you handled?"

Bledsoe laughed. "Don't get your panties in a wad, Sherri. I was making an observation, not a criticism."

"I'll let you know what we find."

She ended the call by dropping the handset into its cradle. When she looked up, she saw Deputy Smith in her doorway.

He didn't say anything about what he'd overheard. Instead he said, "We looked hard at Jolene's stepfather when she first went missing. Maybe we should look at him again."

"Why?"

"There was talk at the time that he was … overly familiar with the girl."

"You couldn't have been involved with all that."

"I was in grade school when she went missing," he admitted. "But I've read the entire case file."

Fine had not. "Give me the condensed version."

Three days after fifteen-year-old Jolene Delacroix disappeared, her mother had filed a missing persons report. When asked why she hadn't reported her daughter's absence sooner, Darlene Wilcox indicated that Jolene had run off before, usually after fighting with her stepfather, but she'd always returned the following day. At first nobody gave her disappearance much attention, but as the days dragged on and she still hadn't returned, sheriff's deputies began asking questions.

"Why our department?" the sheriff asked.

"The family lived about three miles outside of town, so it's a county thing," Smith explained. "Then, as now, Chicken Junction had its haves and its have-nots, and the Wilcoxes—Jolene's mother and stepfather—were clearly among the have-nots, so there was no incentive to pursue the case after talking to the stepfather. A note in the file about Sheriff Danville putting the case on the backburner implies some kind of political pressure to make it go away. At least that's how it looks to me."

Fine had faced similar pressure since becoming sheriff but never over anything as serious as a missing person. "Why are you so interested in this case?"

"My daughter's near about Jolene's age when she disappeared the last time," Smith said. "If anything ever happened to her, I'd want closure. I'm certain Jolene's family does, too."

"They still in the area?"

Smith nodded.

"Let's go talk to them."

When Larry Wilcox opened the door of his mobile home, Sheriff Fine asked, "Mind if we step inside, out of this heat?"

Wilcox moved aside, and the sheriff led Deputy Smith into the living room. Fine and Smith removed their Stetsons before the sheriff said, "We located the remains of your stepdaughter."

Wilcox collapsed onto the couch.

"We're sorry for your loss."

"Somehow, I never thought I would hear those words."

"Where's Mrs. Wilcox?"

"Jolene's mother died a few years back," Wilcox said. "Cancer."

"Must have been hard on her, not knowing what happened to her daughter."

"She wouldn't move out of this house afraid Jolene would come back one day and not be able to find us. I could have gone after Darlene passed away, but in the end, I guess I felt the same way she did." He pushed himself off the couch and led the sheriff down the hall to the back bedroom as he continued. "Jolene's room is just like it was when she left. Darlene wouldn't change anything, and I haven't had the energy to so much as look in here since Darlene passed." He opened the door. "I haven't even dusted."

White nightstands flanked a single bed adorned with a white headboard and pink bedspread. Underneath faded posters of long-forgotten pop stars, a phonograph player with several dozen LPs in the cabinet beneath it occupied the facing wall as did a small white desk that matched the nightstands. A pair of textbooks, an unfinished homework assignment and several pencils remained from Jolene's last use of the desk. The sheriff opened the closet and took stock of the dresses, blouses, and shoes within. Except for the layer of dust coating everything, it appeared as if the dead girl had simply stepped away from her room.

"What about Jolene's father?" Fine asked when she finished examining the girl's bedroom. "We should notify him, but we couldn't find his name in the file."

"Darlene was only sixteen when she birthed Jolene. She wasn't married, and she never told me who the father was."

"So you—"

"I married Darlene when Jolene was four. I raised her like she was my own."

"So why do you think she ran off?"

"Ran off?"

"Her mother said Jolene would leave home after you and she argued," Fine said. "Her mother said it happened frequently."

"Jolene was strong-willed. She didn't like to be told what to do. Anytime I tried, she insisted I wasn't her daddy and that she didn't have to do anything I said."

"That why investigators concentrated their attention on you?"

"They thought I was some kind of freak, interested in my stepdaughter … that way, but I wasn't, not ever." Wilcox took a deep breath and slowly let it out. "Then—then they just stopped coming around. They stopped asking questions. They stopped looking for Jolene and nothing Darlene or I did would make them reopen the investigation."

"There's a note in the files that said your daughter had a boyfriend. There's no name given."

"She never told us who it was."

"And no one came forward."

Wilcox shook his head. "But I'm certain he was older than her."

"Why's that?"

"She once mentioned that he was taking her to dinner over in Quarryville. Can't get there without a car. Not now, and certainly not back then."

They returned to the living room and Fine thanked Wilcox for his time. She told him when and where he could collect the girl's remains for burial.

As the sheriff stepped outside and settled her Stetson into place, Wilcox asked, "You find Jolene's ring?"

Fine turned back to the bereaved man. "Her ring?"

"She never took it off, said it had been her father's."

"I thought she didn't know her father."

"I don't think the ring really belonged to him, but I can't be certain. Darlene gave it to her when she was thirteen."

The sheriff shook her head. "We didn't find it."

Clayton Holms's Senate campaign was in full swing and he was back in Chicken Junction that night for a fund-raising dinner. Though Sheriff Fine wasn't a member of his party, she was obligated to attend the event as Carter Bledsoe's guest. She arrived late to the pre-dinner cocktail reception and found Bledsoe engaged in conversation with a statuesque blonde. Rather than interrupt, she made her way to the open bar and walked away from it gripping a glass of red wine. She circumnavigated the room, making sure to speak, however briefly, with various members of the community's political establishment, until she'd emptied her glass and found herself trapped in a corner with the Senate candidate himself.

"So, you're the young lady who took Garrett's job." His breath reeked of tobacco and red wine.

"Yes, sir, I am."

He shifted position, blocking her view of the rest of the room. "I saw you at my rally. You like what you heard?"

Fine's gaze never left Holms's. "Not in the least."

"You sure are a feisty one." Holms placed his right hand on her left buttock and lowered his voice. "I'll bet you're a lot of fun with your handcuffs when you're not on duty."

"I'm a peace officer and your hand placement is two seconds away from an assault charge."

"Honey, I was district attorney of Arroyo County before you hit puberty." He smiled and squeezed her cheek. "You haven't got the juice to make a charge like that stick."

"How about this then?" Sherri grabbed the candidate's wrist with one hand and with the other bent his fingers back nearly to their breaking point. She stared directly into his eyes and said, "If you ever touch me again, I'll snap your fingers off."

He smiled slowly, but the look in his eyes never changed.

Fine released her grip, stepped around him and made her way to where Bledsoe stood. He'd been watching her, and he asked, "I saw you talking to Holms. What was all that about?"

"A political disagreement," she said.

"Looked like more than that from where I stood."

"We just have different opinions about the 19th Amendment."

When she offered no further explanation, Bledsoe suggested they find their table.

The next afternoon, Sheriff Fine examined the photos she'd taken inside the pole barn before the Chicken Junction crime scene investigator arrived. Dirt appeared disturbed near the remains' left hand. She called Deputy Smith into her office and showed him one of the photos. "I thought you didn't disturb the body."

"I didn't."

"And J.P.?"

"He said he didn't."

"Talk to him again," Fine said. "Somebody did something."

After the deputy left, Sheriff Fine opened Jolene Delacroix's file and read through the witness interviews. She stopped when she came across that of Betty Sue Mayberry. She jotted a note on the scratch pad to her right, adding it to three other names that had caught her interest. All were of women who had attended the same high school as the deceased, and all were within two years of her age. When the sheriff finished, she asked Maybelle, the daytime dispatcher, about the four women.

Maybelle made a few phone calls and reported back that one of the women had died in an automobile accident a few weeks after graduation but that the others still lived in the area.

While Deputy Smith tracked down J.P., Fine went in search of the three women remaining on her list, beginning with the one she'd overheard in the diner the day Jolene's remains were discovered. People in small towns had long memories, and she hoped the case wasn't as cold as it felt.

The woman who answered the door of the small brick ranch had gone doughy with age. The sheriff asked, "Betty Sue Mayberry?"

"I ain't been Mayberry for near on twenty-five years now," said the woman.

"May I come in?"

"You're that lady sheriff, ain't you?"

"Yes, ma'am, I am," Fine said, "and I'd like to ask you a few questions."

"Well, come on in. I'll fix us some sweet tea and you can ask all the questions you like."

Fine followed Betty Sue inside, and soon the two women were sitting at the kitchen table with tall glasses of homebrewed sweet tea before them.

"Now, then, Miss Lady Sheriff, how can I help you?"

"I wanted to ask you about Jolene Delacroix."

"I heard y'all found her. Shame about what happened to that poor girl."

"What exactly did happen, Betty Sue?"

"Well, she died, that's what everybody's saying." Betty Sue lowered her voice and leaned forward, even though they were the only two people in the house. "I even heard that she'd been murdered."

The sheriff didn't confirm the rumor, but neither did she deny it. Instead she said, "You knew her back in high school."

"I did, yes. We weren't friends, but we both lived out from town and rode the same school bus."

"And someone from the sheriff's office talked to you back then, after Jolene disappeared."

"Why, yes, I near forgot about that. Deputy Danville," she said. "I only remember his name because he was elected sheriff a few years later."

"What did you tell him?"

"There wasn't much I could tell," Betty Sue said. "Jolene and me were at school together that day, and she didn't ride the bus home."

"You're certain she wasn't on the bus?"

"I'm positive. She told me someone was picking her up after school."

"Did she say who?"

The doughy woman shook her head.

Everything the sheriff was hearing matched what she'd read in Betty Sue's witness interview, but the handwriting in the report clearly indicated two different interviewers. "The sheriff's not the only one who talked to you, was he?"

Betty Sue brightened. "Oh, no, that was Clayton Holms. He was the district attorney back then. He's the one helped me get the words just right."

Fine sipped her tea and said, "I heard you at the diner say he signed your yearbook. Can you show me?"

"Why, sure thing," Betty Sue said as she stood and disappeared from the kitchen. A moment later she returned with the book in her hands. She opened it to the inside back cover and showed the sheriff what Holms had written. "Imagine, an important man like that taking an interest in a girl like me."

You were my favorite. Clayton

Fine read the words and looked up. "His favorite? Favorite what?"

"A woman got to keep her secrets, Sheriff." Betty Sue smiled coyly as she rested her hand on Fine's forearm. "You ought to know that."

Fine was unable to learn anything more from Betty Sue. She finished her tea, thanked the woman for her time, and drove to the home of the next witness on her list.

Ann Shepherd had different memories of high school and about the day Jolene disappeared.

"You saw Jolene after school that day. Apparently, she didn't ride the bus home. She stayed in town and you saw her later that afternoon."

Ann glanced at the file folder in Sheriff Fine's hand. "If that's what it says."

"You don't remember?"

"That was a long time ago," Ann said. "I've turned my life around, so I try not to think about how things were back then."

"Turned your life around? How?"

"I'd been charged with criminal possession of a controlled substance, and Holms told me he would drop the charges if I swore I saw Jolene after school that day and if I ... if I ..."

Sheriff Fine waited while Ann took a deep breath, calmed herself, and in a deadpan voice described a sexual act.

"I wasn't a virgin," she said, "but I'd never done that. Not before then and never since."

"Why didn't you tell someone?"

"Who could I tell? Who would believe me? I was a poor girl from the wrong side of the tracks, and he was the district attorney!"

The two women sat in silence for a moment.

"So, you didn't really see Jolene after school that day?"

"I said I did, didn't I? Isn't that what your paper says?"

"Sounds like you said it under duress."

Ann shook her head. "I did see her after school, but not at the Dairy Queen. I saw her getting into a car."

"What kind?"

Ann shook her head. "A big one. I don't know cars. A man was driving, but I didn't see his face."

The sheriff found the third witness working at a clothing resale shop. "Laura Jean Melton?"

The slender Clairol-blonde looked the sheriff up and down. "Yes?"

"I'd like to talk to you about Jolene Delacroix."

"I said all I had to say back when she disappeared."

"And what was that?"

"I saw her leaving town in a pickup truck. I didn't recognize the young man driving it."

"What time was that?"

"Must have been after six."

Sheriff Fine glanced at the contents of the file folder she was holding. "That's odd," she said. "I found another witness who says she saw Jolene leaving town right after school, in the company of an older man driving an expensive car."

"No one back then would have said that," she said. "Who changed their story?"

The sheriff didn't answer.

"Look, we did a lot of things back then we shouldn't have," Laura Jean said. "We don't talk about them now."

"Do you know the man who was driving the car?"

"We all did," Laura Jean said. "That's why the sheriff convinced us to say otherwise."

"Who was driving, Ms. Melton?"

Laura Jean shook her head. "But I can tell you this: he liked it rough, Sheriff, and probably still does." She pushed her hair aside and showed Fine the scar on the back of her head. "I needed five stitches."

Deputy Smith returned to the office before Fine and was waiting for her with a clear plastic evidence bag in his hand. He handed it over and said, "J.P. found this near the remains."

The evidence bag contained a Chicken Junction High School class ring dated 1970 inset with a diamond birthstone.

"Looks like a man's ring," Smith said. "It's too big for most women."

Sheriff Fine took the ring to the Wilcox home and showed it to Jolene's stepfather. He said, "It's hers."

"You certain?"

"I ain't seen it in thirty years, but I'm sure," he said as he held the ring up to examine it closer. "Those are her initials scratched inside."

"And your wife told Jolene it was her father's?"

"That's what she said, but my wife worked in a pawn shop, so who's to say if the ring really did come from Jolene's daddy or if Darlene just brought it home because she thought it would make Jolene feel better about herself."

"And did it make Jolene feel better?"

Wilcox nodded. "She thought her daddy was somebody important, more important than me."

The next afternoon, Clayton Holms stepped into the sheriff's office without knocking. Fine looked up and said, "I didn't know you were back in town."

"I'm just passing through, on my way to Quarryville and some of the towns out in that direction. I heard tell you're asking questions about a girl disappeared near on thirty years ago."

"Yes, sir, I am. Turns out you were involved in that same investigation."

"As it was supposed to be," he said. "A good DA knows everything going on in his county, but it seems like you been leaving yours out of the loop this go round."

"When I have something that'll interest Mr. Bledsoe, I'll let him know."

"Oh, honey, you were born with something that interests Carter. That boy's been sniffing around you ever since you started working for him."

The sheriff did not respond to the Senate candidate's lewd suggestion. Instead she said, "Is there something I can do for you?"

"That girl you found," he said. "She ain't worth your time. Everything points to death by misadventure."

"An accident, you mean?"

"There was a group of girls back then, did some foolish things. Surprised more of them didn't come to a bad end."

"How do you mean?"

"The dope, the alcohol, the young men. They all wanted to act like grown-ups and do grown-up things," he said. "We did what we could, the sheriff and me, to guide them in the right direction. They all grew up to be fine women."

"Not all of them."

"How's that?"

"They didn't all grow up."

"Let it rest Sheriff Fine, and I might see to it that you run unopposed next election."

They stared at one another for a moment. The Senate candidate smiled his particular smile, which didn't reach his eyes, and said, "I best be on my way. I heard Quarryville's having an economic resurgence and I want to take a looksee at what they're doing over there."

Sheriff Fine had just poured herself a glass of red wine that evening when she heard a tentative knock on her front door. She opened it to find Ann Shepherd standing on the porch. "May I help you?"

"I'm afraid I wasn't completely honest with you the other day."

"In what way?"

"I know who was driving the car. I seen her with him before. I seen him with other girls, too."

"Who?"

Ann named the former district attorney. "The girls talked to each other. We all knew to avoid him. Well, most of us did. Some of the girls liked the attention, and some of us never had much of a choice."

"You mean—"

"I lived out by the Devil's Canyon Creek cut-off. There's a back way up to the old Latham place, and he liked to take the girls out there. After Jolene disappeared, I never saw his car there again."

"You're suggesting Clayton Holms killed Jolene Delacroix?"

"All I know is what he done to me. I know about the scar on the back of Laura Jean's head. I'm just—I don't know if he done it or not. I just know he could have."

"But why?"

"He got awful rough with me and Laura Jean. Maybe he got rough with her, too—too rough and ..." Anne let her sentence drift off and for a moment she wouldn't meet the sheriff's gaze. "Look, I wouldn't have told nobody else but you. I thought maybe you would understand, not being from here and you a woman and all. I couldn't never have told Sheriff Danville. He's the one who arrested me for possession."

"Was the sheriff getting girls for the DA?"

"No. I don't think so. When Sheriff Danville arrested me, I had the stuff he said I had."

"Will you tell this to the current DA?"

Ann shook her head. "I ain't even sure I should have told you."

Fine reached for her guest's arm. "Can I—"

Ann pulled away. "No. I have to go."

The sheriff couldn't convince Ann to stay and tell her more, and when she found herself alone again, she finished her glass of wine and poured a second.

"I was up to the high school last night to watch Madison in the Spring Choir Concert," Deputy Smith told the sheriff. "Her mama was there with her new boyfriend, so I ducked into the library to avoid having anything to do with them. Did you know they have a copy of every yearbook they ever produced? While I was there, I took a looksee at the class of 1970. Sixty-two boys graduated that year."

"And you're telling me all this because—?"

"Because two stand out—Garrett Danville and Clayton Holms. The sheriff and district attorney were classmates, and they were both involved in investigating Jolene Delacroix's disappearance."

After Deputy Smith left her office, Sheriff Fine phoned the current district attorney and suggested they meet for lunch.

"Your office or mine?"

"Yours," Fine said. Having spent a year as Carter Bledsoe's paralegal and general gofer, she knew his limited culinary palate. "I'll bring Subway."

An hour later she sat in Bledsoe's office, the door closed to prevent eavesdropping. After they'd unwrapped and divided the foot-long tuna sub, she asked, "How well do you know Clayton Holms?"

"I worked for the man for several years before he accepted the judgeship."

"Did you know he liked jailbait?"

Bledsoe's eyes opened wide and the sandwich heading toward his mouth froze in mid-air. "Say what?"

"His wife is twelve years his junior," she explained. She'd spent the time before leaving the office looking into the Senate candidate's background, not as surprised as she'd once been by the amount of information available on the Internet. "He was in his forties when they married, and she was in her twenties."

Bledsoe looked at her. "Why is that important?"

"They first met when she was a teenager and he was leading her church's youth group."

"Nothing happened until they were both adults."

"That's their story," the sheriff said, "but I've talked to a few women who suggest otherwise. They say he paid special attention to the group of them when they were in high school and he was the district attorney."

Bledsoe lowered his sandwich to his section of the waxed paper wrapper. "That's a serious accusation."

"And the statute of limitations for indecency with a minor is long past."

"You're thinking he's good for the Jolene Delacroix thing?"

"I'm thinking I need to look hard at his relationship with the girl."

"That presumes he had one."

"I'm not going to ignore the possibility. I'll keep looking at him until I have a definitive reason not to."

"Your political future should be sufficient reason to let it go," Bledsoe said. "Have you thought about that? If you go public with your suspicions, your political career will be nothing more than buzzard bait. He'll see to that."

"I only have this job because of a fluke," she said. "You really think I'm going to keep it come next election?"

"I was planning to throw my support behind you," Bledsoe said, "but I'm not about to hang your anchor around my neck. You go after Holms and you'll sink for certain."

"I'll go where the evidence takes me, Mr. District Attorney, no matter what happens." She wrapped her uneaten half-sandwich into her napkin and stood. "I think I should return to my own office."

The phone on Sheriff Fine's desk rang. When she answered, Maybelle told her she had a visitor, and a moment later the dispatcher led Jolene Delacroix's stepfather into the sheriff's office. She closed the door and left them to their business.

Sheriff Fine stood. "How may I help you, Mr. Wilcox?"

"My daughter's not coming home, so I started clearing out her room," he said as he handed a pink diary to the sheriff, "and I found this. I think you'll want to read it. I wish I hadn't."

"Why didn't someone turn this in years ago?"

"My daughter hid it up under her nightstand. No one ever thought to search her room for something like this."

The sheriff thanked him and after Wilcox left, she sat down to read.

In a series of entries written in a young girl's purple script, Jolene told her mother's story. She wrote about how one summer afternoon when Garrett Danville and Clayton Holms were home from college, they took her swimming at the abandoned quarry in Quarryville and how, on the way home, they stopped and took turns with her in the back seat of Holms's father's Buick, and about how she'd taken Holms's class ring when he wasn't looking. She couldn't tell anyone what had happened. She knew the young men would tell everyone she'd let them do what they did, and who would believe her word against theirs?

Darlene gave birth to Jolene while the two men were away at college, and she felt certain neither knew her child might belong to one of them. But she did. She just didn't know which one.

A later entry in the diary described Clayton Holms's interest in Jolene's female classmates. She mentioned Betty Sue Mayberry and a few other young women by name. Jolene thought she could use that against him, and she began flirting with Holms until he finally suggested they meet one afternoon. The last entry in the diary, written the morning of the day she disappeared, described her afternoon plans.

Clayton is taking me to the old Latham Ranch after school today. I know what he wants, and when he finishes, I'm going to tell him who I am.

Sheriff Fine phoned the Chicken Junction High School and, when connected with the vice principal, asked if the school retained a record of 1970 class ring purchases. When she found out they did, she asked how many young men had purchased them.

"Only forty-three," the vice principal said, "but one young man purchased a replacement a few years later."

"And who was that?"

Expecting to hear Clayton Holms's name, the sheriff was surprised to hear, "Garrett Danville."

"The former sheriff?"

"One and the same," came the reply. "There's no indication as to what happened to his ring, just that he purchased another one."

"Diamond birthstone?"

"Yes, ma'am. One of only two that year."

Sheriff Fine sat in the district attorney's office and explained to Carter Bledsoe everything she had learned.

When she finished Bledsoe asked, "Could her mother have been confused about whose ring she took?"

"Easily enough. Both men were born in April so both their rings had diamond birthstones," the sheriff said. "But does it really matter? If they both had sex with Jolene's mother, either one could be her father but only one of them killed her."

"And the other helped cover it up."

"That's what it looks like," Fine said.

"So, you think she told him when he finished with her?" Bledsoe asked.

"And led him to believe he'd just fornicated with his own daughter—"

"—even though it could have been his best friend's daughter—"

"—and in a rage, he bashed her head in," the sheriff finished.

"You really think that's what happened?"

"Or something close enough to it. We have means, motive, and opportunity. We have enough for an arrest warrant."

The district attorney sat silently for a long time, just staring at his former paralegal. Finally, he said, "I know a judge who'll sign it."

A few days later Senate candidate Clayton Holms returned to the stage in the Chicken Junction High School gymnasium to address his most loyal supporters, this time under the watchful eye of a trio of cable network news reporters who had noticed his rise in the pre-election polls. Their cameras captured the moment Sheriff Fine and Deputy Smith ascended the stage from opposite sides and approached him.

"Clayton Holms," Fine announced in a voice that carried several rows back without the aid of a microphone. "You're under arrest for the murder of Jolene Delacroix."

SUICIDE INSURANCE

Gerard J Waggett

The last year of my mother's life, I played her numbers every single day. After she died, I still played them, not the daily numbers—she changed those all the time—but the big jackpots: Megabucks, Megamillions, Mass Cash, Cash Winfall. "One of these is going to hit. It's gonna hit big," she promised. My brother Ronan described the lottery as "a state tax for the mathematically impaired." (Yeah, I'd seen that bumper sticker too.) I looked upon the twenty bucks I shelled out each week as suicide insurance. If one of those numbers hit and I wasn't on it, I would borrow Ronan's gun, stick the nozzle in my mouth and *boom!*

Tonight, I was playing my mother's Megamillions numbers: 2-11-14-41-42 with a bonus ball 11. The 2 and 11 represented Ronan, born February 11, 1974. I came along November 14th the same year. (We were Irish twins, and I was premature.) My mother had been 41 when she had Ronan, 42 when she had me. Because the 11 was common to both Ronan and my birthdates, she picked that as her bonus ball. "It's also a lucky number in dice," but she never approved of that sort of gambling.

Before my mother passed away, Megamillions had been called The Big Game, which I still preferred as a title. The lottery machines had not accepted her Big Game slip since the changeover, but I refused to fill out a new one. Most clerks hated taking bets orally, but the old guy running the lottery machine didn't mind. There was no line behind me. There were no other customers anywhere in the entire store. I had checked and doublechecked. Plus, the old guy had been drinking. From the other side of the counter, I could smell the gin on his breath.

A rabbit's foot hung from the side of the lottery machine, the fur gray and white like the old guy's hair but not curly. Before he handed me my ticket, he patted the rabbit's foot against it.

"Do you do that for all your customers?" I asked.

"If I did," he laughed, "that would use up all the luck."

Ronan was half-sitting on the hood of my Volvo. Although we were Irish twins, people used to mistake us for the real thing, partly because our mother had held Ronan back so that he and I could go to school together. Now he looked a good ten years older than me, and it wasn't just that his hair was thinning. He had spent six of his thirty-eight years behind bars.

"He's all alone." I should have added, *Go easy, he's a nice guy.*

Ronan pulled a handgun out of the ski mask he was holding, then pulled the ski mask over his face.

No sooner had I slid into the driver's seat, I heard the pop. It had come from inside the store. In the neighborhood where Ronan and I now lived, you heard that pop more than once a week. Up here in the enchanted forests of the North Shore, you might never hear it. If you did, you would probably mistake the sound for thunder or your neighbor's SUV backfiring, maybe a firecracker left over from the Fourth of July.

Ronan came running out, his gun in one hand, a bottle in the other.

In one ear-piercing squeal, my car arced backwards into the unlit road. We were nearing eighty miles an hour when Ronan ordered me to slow down and turn on the headlights. Too many of the inmates he'd met had been caught while pulled over for stupidity like speeding and failing to signal. The first time Ronan himself had been arrested, the police had tracked him down through a parking ticket, "four quarters I should have shoved into the friggin' meter."

We stopped at the bridge, for me to piss and Ronan to toss his gun into the river. He didn't care if it washed up on the shore; he didn't care if it washed up on the steps of the police station. It could not be traced back to him.

"What happened back there?" I finally asked.

The old guy had thrown a bottle at Ronan. When Ronan ordered him to open the register, he grabbed a bottle of brandy from the shelf behind him and flung it at Ronan's head. "It damn near hit me too. How stupid do you have to be?" he asked. "Gun versus bottle. Who would you bet on?"

Gun, obviously, "but I think he was kinda drunk."

Roman thanked me "for the heads up." He did not know where he had shot the guy, only that the guy had dropped immediately down, at which point Ronan grabbed a bottle and ran.

We did not discover until the next morning that Ronan had killed the man, who was not a clerk but the owner, Frank Fessi. Ronan had shot him in the face.

"I was aiming for the bottle. He had picked up another one to throw at me."

Ronan hadn't mentioned a second bottle before now, but I chose to believe him.

The early morning news had cut to a live report from the parking lot of Fessi's Liquor store, which had been "a family business since just after World War II. The victim leaves behind a wife Linda and two sons, aged four and six." In the photo "from a family vacation this past summer," Frank looked like the boys' grandfather.

Our father had been older as well. He died when Ronan and I were eight and seven. Two days after Christmas, he was shoveling snow with Ronan, and dropped dead, massive coronary. I had been inside the house, baking cookies with my mother. I felt bad for Frank's sons, as I'm sure Ronan did as well, but growing up without a father would not have been any easier on them if he died from natural causes.

Ronan aimed the remote at the TV just as the blonde anchorwoman announced: "These are last night's winning Megamillions numbers …"

"Hold on," I said. In all the confusion last night, I had not yet checked them.

2 – 11 – 14 – 41 – 42 and another 11 stretched across the TV screen. The second 11 had been circled in red.

Even Ronan recognized them. "Aren't those ma's—?"

"Yes," I laughed, "they are." I stared until the numbers disappeared, replaced by a commercial for a luxury car I could finally afford.

Ronan muted the set. "How much …?"

The jackpot was 142 million, "but you don't get all that."

"How much do you get?" he wanted to know.

"If you're the only winner and you take the lump sum, after taxes, you end up with about a third."

"A third of 142 million."

"Thirty-seven million." Despite what the bumper sticker claimed, I could add, subtract, multiply and divide.

"This calls for a toast." Ronan, who normally would have sent me into the kitchen for glasses, got up to fetch them himself.

While he did, I looked around at the apartment for what I hoped would be one of the very last times. For two years, ever since his parole, Ronan and I had been crammed into this place, which had been barely big enough for me alone. For two years, he had been sleeping on the couch, finishing off my beer and dominating the TV set. I could walk out the door right this very second and never come back. I could check myself and Ronan into one of those fancy hotels on the waterfront, but in separate rooms, on separate floors, maybe even in separate hotels.

Ronan plopped two scratched up juice glasses on an even more scratched up coffee table. Later on today, he and I would toast our good fortune properly, with French champagne, not stolen scotch.

Ronan lifted his glass, which he had filled higher than mine. "To my rich brother …"

"And to Ma." Even from beyond the grave, she was looking after her boys.

Ronan raised the glass to his lips, then paused. "Bobby, are you absolutely, positively sure you played the number?"

"Absolutely, positively." I could have showed him the ticket, it was still in my back pocket, but something in the back of my mind warned me not to let him touch it. "I played it last night."

Ronan put down his glass unsipped. Experts considered that bad luck, not that he believed in luck, good or back, although after today, maybe he might.

"Did you play that number at Fessi's?"

"Yeah." Hadn't I just told him that?

Ronan exploded with one of the only two swears my mother never allowed in her house. "Bobby," he said, "we can't cash that ticket."

"Don't tell me you suddenly believe in karma."

That he didn't. "The tickets are coded. The numbers across the bottom—they tell the store and the time when it was bought."

I had worked in convenience stores. I knew that.

"If we cash in that ticket," he explained, "we're putting ourselves at the liquor store right when Frank Fessi got shot."

"But it doesn't prove that I shot him." I held myself back from adding, *because you did*. "And they probably have me on the security camera."

"But they don't know who you are." Before we started all this, Ronan had told me not to worry about the camera; with a baseball cap, I looked like a million other guys. "Once they have your name, the police will investigate till they find something. They will sweep every inch of your car."

"There's nothing to find. You threw away the gun, and the only other thing would be that …" I pointed to the scotch bottle. "And you've pretty much gotten rid of that evidence."

"They'll find something small, something we don't even know means anything. They'll look at my record, and they'll know it was us, and they won't stop till they prove it." Ronan shifted into that soft, almost pleading tone he had reserved only for our mother. "Bobby, you have to get rid of that ticket."

"You know you're getting a cut, right?" I wouldn't split the ticket down the middle, but I planned on giving him two, maybe three million.

The money wasn't swaying him. "Trust me as someone who's been there, after one night in prison, you would give up the entire thirty-seven million to be free, but by that point, it will be too late."

Before this discussion deteriorated into a knock-down drag-out, I wanted to double-check that I had actually won this jackpot. We lived three floors above the convenience store where I usually played my numbers and where I should have played them last night, but I couldn't just walk into Fessi's and stand there without a reason. Playing the numbers, reading each one out loud gave me time to case the place.

Tony, the clerk, printed me out a slip with the winning Megamillions numbers: 2-11-14-41-42, bonus ball 11

When Tony saw the look on my face, he wished me, "Better luck tonight. Powerball's over two hundred million."

On my way up the stairs, I checked the numbers yet again. They hadn't changed. I was walking around with 142 million dollars in my back pocket.

When I let myself into the apartment, Ronan was coming out of my bedroom. We looked at each other for a solid moment but didn't say anything. I didn't need to ask what he'd been looking for.

An idea had come to me on the stairs. "What if we got someone to cash the ticket for us?"

Ronan laughed. "Who do we know that we could trust?"

"Ellen."

"Your *ex*-wife."

She had not screwed me over in the divorce. She would not screw me over now. She would want a piece of the winning, but she would not steal it all.

That Ronan did not argue, "but would she lie to the cops for us? They will question her as a possible witness."

That she could not do, not convincingly anyway. The last time we talked, Ellen had just been promoted to office manager at a law firm downtown.

"Which means what?" Ronan asked, "She sharpens pencils and pays the phone bill?"

Whatever she did there, she worked for lawyers who handled some pretty serious criminals. "With this kind of money," I said, "we could hire one of them."

"If this was just robbery," Ronan said, "I'd take my chances. But this is murder."

The way Ronan had described it, it sounded to me like self-defense.

"Not during a hold-up."

Ronan didn't trust lawyers, and I couldn't blame him. The last time he was arrested, our mother mortgaged the house to hire a lawyer. She refused to entrust her son's freedom to another public defender. "But I would have been better off with a public defender," he said. "A public defender would have pushed me into cutting a deal." The lawyer our mother hired, from the firm of Arrogant, Overconfident, and Incompetent, convinced Ronan that he could walk away without any jail time. Thanks to him, Ronan was sentenced to three years more than the deal had offered, and Ma lost her house.

I did not need to be reminded. Every day I woke up in this apartment reminded me. "But the lawyers Ellen works for are better."

"No," Ronan said, "they just charge more."

"You would recognize the mobsters they've gotten off." He had probably served time with some of their henchmen. "And that doctor from Mass General who killed his wife ...? He's still practicing medicine."

While I had been downstairs getting the printout, I was not the only one thinking up new arguments. "You could do a lot of good with that money, Bobby. You could donate it to that orphanage you give to every Christmas, the Home for Little .... Vagabonds?"

"Wanderers." Somewhere I had written up a list of all the charities I'd remember when I hit the big jackpot, and they were already on it.

Ronan, who used to cuff bills from the collection plate at church, was now advocating that I give the entire thirty-seven million dollars to this orphanage, anonymously. "Or what about Frank Fessi's family? Under the circumstances, who deserves that jackpot more than his wife and kids?"

"Me," I said. I planned to set up some trust fund for those boys, but I wasn't going to give them thirty-seven million because my idiot brother had shot their father. I wouldn't give them the whole jackpot if I had shot their father myself.

Ronan stood up for the next argument. "The way Frank Fessi was killed, the lottery might not have to honor your ticket."

"Says who? I bought the ticket."

"While casing the place. That makes it part of the crime."

"I need a nap." I was exhausted. I had been up all night, but I was also too excited to sleep. All I really needed was a door between me and Ronan.

I had not been in my room more than twenty minutes before Ronan was knocking. "Not now," I shouted, prompting him to bang all that much harder. He wouldn't tire, he wouldn't quit. He would only get louder. I tied my shoe and pulled the door open.

"I don't want to hear anymore—"

The bottle clipped me right in the mouth. If Ronan hadn't drunk all the scotch, the weight of it would have knocked out my front teeth.

"That is how they'll welcome you your first night in prison. You don't want to know what they will do with the other end." He held the bottle by the bottom so I could get a close look at the neck.

Before I could tell him that rich people didn't go to prison, he body slammed me into the door frame. His free hand slid into my back pocket. Before holding up corner stores and breaking into drugstores, Ronan had picked pockets. He'd started when he was twelve and frustrated himself no end, trying to teach me.

His index finger ordered me to stay put while he fished through my wallet. He laughed at the picture on my license before dropping it and my bank card onto the ground. He crumpled up two receipts and tossed them into my bedroom. The ten-dollar bill and three singles he stuffed into his own pocket. Behind the picture of our mother, he found the slip, folded in half, and then quartered.

"Please," I cried. "We have a year to cash it in. We can figure something out."

"This is dangerous." Ronan pinched the wad between his index and middle fingers. "This will send us to prison."

"Ronan—"

"You could have done some good with this money, Bobby. You could have helped out that orphanage. You could have helped out Frank Fessi's orphans. Instead ...?" Ronan popped the wad into his mouth.

I cupped my hand and held it under his mouth. "Seriously."

Ronan slapped my hand away and kept chewing. He chewed with his mouth wide open, daring me to stick my fingers inside. The wad caught in his throat. He washed it down with the scotch he had poured for our toast.

"You just swallowed thirty-seven million dollars."

Ronan patted his stomach. "This was *my* suicide insurance. I will kill myself before I go back to prison."

I picked my wallet up off the floor along with the bank card and license. My mother's numbers were sitting on top of my dresser. "I need to play these," I told Ronan.

He handed me the empty scotch bottle. "Get rid of this while your out."

I had never expected him to eat the ticket he found. I figured that he would rip it into thirty-seven million pieces or set fire to it with the stove, maybe burning down the apartment building in the process. I didn't care. I was never going back there.

When he found the printout hidden behind the picture of our mother, I trusted that he wouldn't inspect it, not too closely. It was a gamble, but sometimes they paid off.

The Lottery's main headquarters was located down in Braintree. I had mapped out the route in anticipation of this day.

Bill Clepp, the agent I met with, looked so sharp in his grey wool suit and maroon silk tie, I apologized for my sweatshirt and jeans. I really wanted to wear my one good suit, the one I'd bought for my mother's funeral, but I could not have walked past Ronan wearing that.

I sat down and took off my right shoe. Bill smiled as he watched me pull out the ticket. "It's not the oddest hiding spot I've ever seen."

"Were there any other winners last night?" I didn't want to split the thirty-seven million in half (eighteen point five), or three ways (twelve and a third).

"That won't affect you," Bill said. "We only split the jackpots."

"That is the jackpot."

Bill compared the ticket to a printout on his desk. "I'm sorry, but you need *all* five numbers plus the bonus ball."

I had been playing the lottery for almost twenty years. What I didn't need was the rules explained to me. "I have all five numbers: two, eleven, fourteen—"

"You don't have the fourteen." Bill passed the ticket back to me so I could inspect it for myself:

2-11-40-41-42, bonus ball 11.

In all the confusion after the shooting and then hiding the ticket from Ronan this morning, I had never looked at the ticket until right then. I had glanced at it as I was putting it into my shoe, but then Ronan started banging on my door.

Frank Fessi, who had been drinking on the job, must have heard for*ty*, forty-one, forty-two, not four*teen*, forty-one, forty-two. My mother would have called this an honest mistake, but I didn't see it that way at all. If Frank Fessi had run down a child while driving home drunk last night, the parents wouldn't forgive him for making an honest mistake.

Bill Clepp was jabbering on about taxes now. The final figure he'd come up with, sixty-six hundred dollars and change, would not pay for the level of lawyer I needed. It didn't come close. You couldn't pay off a judge or bribe jurors with $6600. You couldn't post bail and flee the country to anyplace decent.

Bill had pulled forms from the drawer to his right. Before the lottery could cut me a check, I needed to fill them out.

"It's not worth it."

"It's not worth ten thousand dollars?"

"It's not even the full ten thousand," I pointed out and asked for my ticket back.

Before I left the man's office, I asked if I could play the lottery anywhere in the building. I had my mother's numbers with me along with a ten-dollar winner I'd need to cash in to play them. Maybe my mother's numbers would be lucky here, this place being the source. The numbers definitely would have been played correctly here. And if just one of them hit for more than a million dollars, I wouldn't need to drive my car into the side of the building. ☛

THE POWER OF THE DOG

Leone Ciporin

If Rufus hadn't licked my cheek, I wouldn't be standing onstage in a dog suit with sweat trickling down my neck. The pants aren't bad, but the black and white top is heavy and the head only lets in air through mesh eyes. The tail keeps swishing, so I grip it, feeling like the Cowardly Lion. At least I don't have to smile. Chester the Shelter Dog comes with a plastic grin.

"Ladies and gentlemen." The mayor's smile blossoms his ruddy cheeks, making him look more like a chipmunk than usual. "Welcome to the Mansfield County Animal Shelter's first annual Furry Friends Festival." With each f, he rat-a-tats globules of spit into the crowd.

Two women in the front row wipe their foreheads. Behind them, teens whisper, kids slurp and at the very back, a skinny man in a faded red shirt elbows an elderly lady. I try to spot my brother Brendan, who's watching Rufus. I catch a glimpse of Brendan's strawberry blond hair.

The county park, a rare flat space in the Blue Ridge Mountains, is overrun by funnel cake trucks, cotton candy stands and pet product booths, surrounded by trees waving green leaves alongside orange and gold specks.

Behind the crowd, vendors shout, dogs bark and groups laugh, making it hard to hear the mayor as he repeats, "Ladies and gentlemen."

Definitely more ladies, most with kids or dogs. Near the front, a woman with a collie stands next to a Kool-Aid splattered mom juggling two toddlers. Behind them, teenage girls stare at a boy sauntering past. The smattering of men includes the Kool-Aid mom's husband, a white-haired man holding a giant soda and the thin man with the red shirt, who's weaving his way through the crowd.

The weather is perfect, just the right blend of summer and fall, the hot sun balanced by breezy air as crispy as a Triscuit. We only get a few such days each year, and I'm giving up part of this one for the sauna of a dog suit.

The mayor adjusts the lapel of his sport coat. "To open, Mrs. Wilkins's kindergarten class will present Chester the Shelter Dog with a check."

That's my cue. I wave a paw, wishing I could use it to wipe the sweat now rolling down my back. Paul would laugh if he could see me. He's the one who's going to a four-year school instead of community college, who has a part-time job at an office instead of a preschool, who's better than me at everything and knows it. After I adopted Rufus, I got tired of being treated like second best by anyone else.

A toddler bursts from the crowd, the Kool-Aid husband sprinting after him. In front of them, the red-shirted man stares intently at me, his jaw sliding from side to side like it's about to unhinge. I'm glad the costume hides my face.

"The children raised money for the shelter by selling crafts they made." The mayor sweeps a hand toward the class.

Mrs. Wilkins hasn't aged well in the thirteen years since I was in her class. Back then, she was like a cheerful, slightly distracted big sister, who said I had a gift for empathy, a word I had to ask my parents to explain. She looks old now, with her wrinkled maxi-skirt and sturdy sandals.

Then she sprints after a wandering black-haired boy, her yell, "Sweetie! Come back!" snapping me into a memory I've kept, crystal clear, like a snow globe.

When we had to put down our beagle, I couldn't talk in class all week. Once Mrs. Wilkins got me to tell her about it, she brought in a Rudyard Kipling poem called The Power of the Dog, about how a dog can tear at your heart, and read me the part about "when the body that lived at your single will, with its whimper of welcome, is stilled (how still!)." I learned to read on that poem.

Mrs. Wilkins catches the black-haired boy just before he reaches the lip of the stage. "Sebastian, get back with the group."

A girl with wheat-colored hair spiraling down her back pulls Sebastian into the cluster. I know that girl. She was in my preschool last year, and I feel bad that I can't think of her name.

"Thank you, Hayley," Mrs. Wilkins says. Good old Mrs. Wilkins, helping me out again.

I wave a paw at Hayley, who waves back.

The mayor hands Mrs. Wilkins a cardboard check and shuffles offstage. The crowd claps. Brendan waves.

Brendan's only a year behind me, so he was there when I met Paul the night our high school lost the homecoming game last year, our brown and gold banners overrun by green and white. A tall boy in a green cashmere sweater walked up, his smile spotlighting a dimple, and said, "You're too pretty to wear brown and gold." Then Paul reached around my kid brother to wrap me in a green blanket. I stared at Brendan's thick jacket, and pulled Paul's blanket tight around me. It was the wrong color, but it protected me from the callous chill.

When we got home, Brendan said I shouldn't go out with Paul. I teased that he just hated losing the game, and he said, "I'm not a sore loser. But I have a feeling Paul would be."

Brendan is laughing at something now. I can't see Rufus. The Kool-Aid toddlers are deep into their sippy cups, while two small dogs sniff each other.

The red-shirted man is in the front row, a muscle under his cheek jumping in time to pop music wafting from a booth. He fingers a lump at his waist. My heart pings an alarm.

I step forward. Then I remember I'm not Emma, the good girl who keeps everything in order. I'm Chester the Shelter Dog, who waves, but doesn't speak. I step back.

Mrs. Wilkins extends the cardboard check toward me. She's wearing a shelter button. I want to tell her it's me inside the costume, but I just grab the check and wiggle Chester's tail. Rufus is the expert wiggler, his back end whipping so fast he sometimes trips himself. I do the best I can, making the children giggle and the crowd laugh. Except the red-shirted man.

"Children," Mrs. Wilkins leans the check against the stage. "Let's tell Chester how much we love him."

Hayley steps forward, beaming. "C is for cute!"

Sebastian stomps up and shouts, "H is for happy!"

A pudgy boy whose collar needs straightening shuffles forward. "E is for—"

Screams slice off his sentence. The red-shirted man is onstage, brandishing a handgun.

Every movement comes in inches. A white noise buzzes in my ears and my feet feel frozen, but I see clearly. Even the man's sweat stains are clear. I smell his salty odor from the other side of the stage. He's screaming, but the buzzing in my ears drowns out his words.

The world speeds up to real time, and the noise of running feet and panicked screams replaces the buzzing. The crowd is running away, but Mrs. Wilkins, the children and I are trapped onstage.

Mrs. Wilkins steps between the gunman and her class. "Calm down," she says in the voice she once used to console me. She holds up a hand as a stop sign.

The gun shakes. "You killed my dog." His voice rumbles like a truck over gravel. "You killed Ranger." He's staring at her button with the shelter logo.

His face contorts. The gun goes off. Mrs. Wilkins crumples.

I run toward her, but the man grabs Hayley and lifts her like a shield, his gun against her curls. I screech to a halt, mere inches from him. Below the man's stubbled chin, Hayley's eyes stare at Chester, and past the mesh into my eyes.

"Stay," the man commands me. "Stay."

He sees Chester, not Emma. I don't know what to do. Where is Brendan? If he were onstage, he'd tackle the man. But I'm not Brendan. I'm not even Chester.

"Stay," the gunman says again. Over his shoulder, two men reach onto the stage and yank Mrs. Wilkins off. Her hand wiggles as she disappears. She's alive. I relax stomach muscles I didn't remember clenching.

"Get back there with those kids," the red-shirted man says. "Get back there, dog."

I join the huddle of children crowded against the back of the stage. They wrap themselves around my legs, piling on each other to get to me, stroking Chester's fur, petting me all over. One child grips my leg so tightly my calf cramps.

I crouch, releasing the cramping grip, and hold out Chester's paws. The children stuff themselves between the furry arms, or lean on my back and shoulders. I need the hugs as much as they do. We rock back and forth, the smell of funnel cake on one boy's breath mingling with the smell of urine.

I whisper into the huddle, "C is for ..."

A boy with baggy cargo shorts whispers, "Cute."

"H is for ..."

Sebastian says, "Happy."

The red-shirted man hollers at police cars filing into the park. "Ranger loved me! He loved me and one of you killed him. Which one of you did it? I'll make you pay." His voice softens. "Ranger was so sweet."

I stretch my costume neck to search for Rufus, but all I see is police.

Brendan was the one who found Rufus, a reddish pit bull trotting along the highway. When Brendan pulled over, the dog laid his head in Brendan's palm. After he told me, I drove to the shelter to see the dog. Just to see him.

But Rufus looked up with those big eyes, and I had to take him for a walk. He tried to climb into my lap, though he was so big I could almost have climbed into his. He gave me a wide pit bull grin and his tongue swiped my cheek.

"You win," I told him. "You're mine."

"You killed Ranger!" The man's yell comes out as a thin screech. "He was just doing a dog's job, stopping that man from taking my home. I was born in that house!" His sob whistles into a wail. "Ranger was my best friend!"

I hurt for him, until he swivels, revealing Hayley. Her eyes are closed.

"Which one of you killed Ranger?" he screams. "Where are you?"

I'm pretty sure I know who did it. When I adopted Rufus, I asked the woman at the front desk what would have happened to him if I hadn't come along.

She said, "We save most animals that come here. Some we have to put down for medical reasons or because they're a danger." Her mouth twisted. "None of us want to do that to an animal." When she handed me a volunteer brochure, I took it.

The children crowd closer, nearly knocking my costume head sideways. Inside the cocoon of Chester's head, my breath boomerangs against my cheeks. I pat and squeeze to comfort the children. I'd be their Rufus. Love unflinching, like the Kipling poem said. After I brought Rufus home, I dug up that poem, yellowy and dry, and pinned it to my refrigerator.

A chill wiggles up my back as I recall the verse on when "the vet's unspoken prescription runs to lethal chambers or loaded guns." I know this gun is loaded.

The man's shadow passes over us as he paces, screaming at the growing number of police cars. "You took my dog—I'll take your kid!" He leans the gun against Hayley's hair. But he isn't paying attention to the other children at all. And he never noticed Mrs. Wilkins being pulled away. Maybe I can get the children offstage without him noticing.

I count. Fourteen. Fourteen little souls yearning to grow into bigger souls. Maybe I can keep them safe.

Maybe I can't. Maybe I don't know what I'm doing.

No. That's Paul's voice. The voice I heard the night I blurted out my plan for a master's degree in counseling. Paul turned to the waiter, ordering steak, medium rare, for both of us, though I was uncomfortable eating creatures with soft eyes.

Once the waiter left, Paul smiled just wide enough to pucker his dimple. "I don't think you need a master's degree to deal with little kids."

"Preschool is just part-time. I'm talking about a career."

"I'd hate for you to study so hard for nothing. You should enjoy yourself."

I kept my courage by picturing Rufus's adoring eyes, his complete trust in me. "I need support, not criticism."

Paul scribbled a signature on the credit card slip. "I'm just looking out for you.

Call me when you're ready to listen."

"But you're not listening to me."

After a startled silence, Paul tossed a twenty at me. "Get a cab." Three days later, when I hadn't apologized, he called to announce it was over.

I need the confidence that helped me stand up to him, to take the risk of being alone. That voice tells me I can save these children.

But how? Maybe I can drop them behind the stage. I push against the tarp, but it's pinned too tightly to slip even a child through. I have to go around.

I stand slowly, my legs stiff. The children pull at me, trying to keep me down with them. I hold a paw to Chester's mouth for silence, grab Sebastian and the boy with sagging cargo shorts and pull them behind me.

As I take a few steps, the other children follow, but I signal them to stay put. With the two boys grabbing fistfuls of fur at my back, I start sidling to the edge of the stage, glancing at the gunman every few steps. He fidgets, but the closest police car has all his attention. A bald officer speaks softly, so softly I can barely hear, except for a few words like fine, calm and let's talk.

"Ranger was a good dog," the man tells the bald cop in a lullaby voice. "He looked after me when I was sick, even lay on top of me when I got the shivers."

The night Paul broke up with me, Rufus climbed onto my lap, his legs splaying, and rested his cheek against mine.

I blink back tears and inch closer to the corner of the stage. Step. Another step. I slow down to stop Chester's paws from slapping the stage. Only a few steps left. I try to see the corner of the stage through the mesh eyes, but it's too hard to do that and move at the same time, so I keep shuffling.

The boys' hands vanish and I glimpse an arm. I trot back to the other children, stopping only to grab Chester's tail when it starts flapping in the wind.

One girl is crying. I drop immediately. "E is for …"

The pudgy boy with the uneven collar says: "E is for excellent."

I ruffle his hair. "S is for …" The pause tells me S is safely off stage. I want to make a fist pump.

A girl with a cockeyed pink barrette finally whispers, "S is for super."

The pudgy boy nudges her. "It's shelter." She actually giggles.

Twelve left. Six trips, if I take two each time. I don't dare risk taking them all at once. Even police cars wouldn't distract him from that.

But if I take three at a time, that's only four trips, four times he might catch us. I have to try. It's up to me to keep them safe, just as it was my job to keep Brendan safe. My brother expected the world to take care of him and my parents expected me to make that happen. Brendan was always looking for adventure, and our parents kept telling me to watch out for him. Which mainly meant saying don't climb that tree, don't walk on that rickety fence, don't, don't, don't.

I want to tell myself don't. Don't take that next trip. Don't draw the attention of the man with the gun. As I think about making that shuffle again, my pulse throbs and my breath stops and starts.

I look around for some other way out. News vans are parked between the cluster of police and the rubbernecking crowd beyond. I can't see Brendan or Rufus in that crowd. How long has it been? It feels like just a few minutes, but also like life has never been any other way.

The bald cop starts talking again. Though the cop's head is shaved, his face is smooth. He's young. His megaphone hangs at his side and he speaks softly, in a rise-and-fall rhythm. "Lyle," he says. "We can work this out. We can fix this."

Lyle. Finally, the gunman has a name. It makes him less intimidating, just another person, who can be reasoned with. I look closely at him. His shirt hem is frayed and his thick, brown hair is layered, but matted, like it was tended to once, but not now.

Lyle's gun shakes. It looks heavy. His sentences come between gulps. He tells the cop, "I found Ranger as a puppy. Someone dumped him like trash. Who would do that to a little bitty puppy?" He bends his cheek to Hayley's hair, the gun still against her head. "Who would be so mean?"

Sometimes at night, I trace the scars on Rufus's nose or finger the notch in his ear, and imagine the torture I'd inflict on whoever made those marks. I'd kiss the notch over and over, as if that would mend it.

Lyle raises his head. "Ranger used to roll over and grin at me and I'd give him belly rubs." His face cracks into a smile. "He loved belly rubs, he'd let me rub him all day."

Rufus likes standing belly rubs. He leans into me and licks my cheek while I pat his back with one hand and rub his belly with the other.

Lyle's mouth trembles into a pout. "Now I'm alone again. No one to talk to … I loved him so much."

I know that feeling, that heart tear, what the poem calls "love unflinching." It's a powerful thing. And I feel it now for the children. I have to take the next three.

I hold Chester's head with one hand to keep it from tipping while I look down at the children around my legs. They look up with Rufus-like expressions, their trust total and pure. And I have to choose.

I choose a girl whose porcelain cheeks are trembling, and two more girls with arms intertwined. We shuffle more slowly with three children instead of two, but the hands behind the stage are quicker this time, the girls' grip loosening almost before I reach the edge.

When I come back, a brawny boy pushes a smaller boy aside to get to me. I remember him from last year's preschool class. Dale had a tendency to shove, but I set consistent boundaries and his behavior improved.

I find myself doing it again, waving him away as punishment, praying the penalty won't be death. I point at a girl with blonde pigtails and two boys with rigid stares that seem about to crumble.

I spread my arms and the three children take their positions behind me. We begin our shuffle. Step, step, step. I can almost see the lip of the stage. I sniffle to reverse a runny nose.

Lyle glances our way. I cock my head the way Rufus does when he's done something questionable. Lyle hesitates. His gun moves up and down against Hayley's head, like he's using it to brush her hair.

The bald officer squawks through the megaphone. "Stand down. Drop your weapon." Lyle whips away to scream at the cop. I deliver the children safely and scoot back to the dwindling class. Six left. Two trips.

The girl with the pink barrette squinches up for another cry. I lean into the circle. "T is for?"

A somber girl says, "T is for terrific."

A boy with thick glasses pipes in. "E is for extra-special."

And R?" I ask. Silence. R is safe. I touch barrette girl's nose.

She whispers, "R is for rescue."

A tiny sob pops from my mouth.

On my next trip, I choose Dale, the boy he shoved and the girl with the cockeyed barrette. As we inch toward rescue, my nose itches. I reach to scratch it, and bang Chester's plastic nose instead.

Lyle spins around. "Get back there." He points to the cluster of children. He doesn't seem to notice there are less of them.

He's facing me and I see Hayley clearly. Her eyes are open now. Her lip quivers, but she's not crying. She never cried in preschool, no matter what. She was always the helper, never the one helped.

One Monday, after a fight with Paul, I kept dropping books and spilling grape juice. When I knocked over a box of crayons, I stared at the floor to keep from crying, and saw a chunky hand picking up crayons. By the time Hayley put them all back, I'd defeated my tears.

Now she dangles in a gunman's grip.

I try not to look at Hayley as I lead the other children back to the group. I'm grateful she doesn't know it's me. I let myself be distracted by sweat and itches.

I cuddle the six children left, crooning, "I'm sorry. I know it's scary." My shirt itches from sweat and I feel a tinge of satisfaction in not scratching.

As Lyle patrols the stage, one shoelace lagging behind, a tear runs down his cheek and I think of the poem: "I bid you beware, Of giving your heart to a dog to tear."

The bald cop starts talking again. He cradles the megaphone in one brawny arm and his tone is gentle. "Lyle, I know you miss Ranger." Does he really understand how a dog tears at your heart?

Lyle starts crying, his nose filling with bubbles. "I was so lonely before Ranger." His sniff pops the bubbles. "I'd just sit in my room. No one to talk to!" He leans toward the cop, swinging Hayley's feet. I look away from her little white tennis shoes.

Lyle gets that dreamy tone again. "Ranger loved tennis balls. I'd throw them and he'd run so hard, he'd trip sometimes. But he'd catch that ball and bring it back to me."

Rufus loves tennis balls too, but he hates to let go. He tucks the ball into the corner of his mouth, wrinkling his cheek. He looks like an old man with a cigar.

There's a scuffle, as a reporter tries to advance past the police cordon. Most of the officers crouch behind cars angled in vees. Inside one vee, a miniature stuffed Chester lays on his side, half his grin buried in the grass.

All the cops are watching Lyle, except the one with the megaphone. He looks straight at me. Waiting for a signal.

Keeping an eye on the megaphone cop, I grab three children—I'm not sure which—and pull them behind me. I press them into my back with my paws and we start shuffling. My cop friend gives a small nod and shifts his attention to Lyle. He'll distract him if needed.

As we shuffle across, a rebellious thought crawls into my mind. Brendan couldn't do this. He'd tackle Lyle, and get shot. Brendan couldn't stay unnoticed. I do that all the time.

We reach the edge of the stage and the children vanish. I stop for a moment, sweat streaming down my body, so tired I want to collapse in a heap right on the stage.

I return to the last three children, as Lyle yells, "You killed him just like I could kill that dog there. For a moment, I think he means me and I freeze. What will happen to Rufus if I die?

But he aims the gun at the stuffed Chester on the ground. He shifts his hand at the last moment before blasting, deliberately missing the stuffed dog.

Cops shout, people scream and the megaphone blares. Lyle's gun is on Hayley's head again. "I don't kill dogs," he tells the police. "You do."

The children start crying. I clutch them. Lyle paces the front of the stage, stomping on tiptoe like a child wanting to run.

The bald cop leans his megaphone against his shoulder. "Lyle, you don't want to hurt anyone, especially a child."

"He shot my dog!"

The cop says, "Todd ..." His hand grips the megaphone, then loosens. "Deputy Clayton was just trying to do his job. He wasn't trying to hurt anyone."

Lyle's cheek throbs. "He shot my Ranger. Ranger wouldn't have hurt him if he'd left us alone. He weren't no pit bull." I want to slap that twitchy cheek.

I have to focus on the last trip. The last three children. The solemn-faced girl, the boy with glasses and a chubby girl with strands of hair escaping her headband. Though she's the last to be rescued, the chubby girl looks up and lifts the corners of her mouth, like she needs only the slightest excuse to break into a smile.

I touch their shoulders and they immediately step behind me. I nod at the megaphone cop, as his collar ruffles in the breeze, and I wish I were there with him, standing in that breeze, turning over responsibility, no one depending on me to save them.

We begin our shuffle. Two steps, four, six. The stage edge comes into view. Just a few more shuffles.

"Lyle, put the girl down." I jump as the megaphone squawks. The children jump too, pressing against my arms.

Lyle stares at me, his nostrils widening and narrowing as if he's trying to catch my scent. But the megaphone blares again and Lyle turns toward the cop, who drops the megaphone and says, "Lyle, we can work this out."

Lyle pivots toward him, listening to the soothing rhythm. We shuffled again, with the last megaphone blast—"put the girl down"—reverberating in my head.

Hayley. I need to save Hayley. As if she hears my thoughts, Hayley starts crying. The girl who never cries blubbers as Lyle jabs the gun at her ear. "I want to meet the monster who killed my dog," he says. "Give me the dog killer and you can have your kid back."

I know he means the deputy, but I keep thinking of the woman at the shelter, the one with kind eyes. But I'd still trade her for Hayley.

A child's panting breath in my ear reminds me to focus. Just a few more steps.

The chubby girl stumbles with a thump. The megaphone squawks, but it's too late.

"Get back over there!" Lyle waves Hayley like a second weapon.

We're so close. I help the girl to her feet and her body shakes under my paws. I can't send them back.

I wave at the children to run, blocking his view as much as I can. As soon as they disappear behind the stage, I walk toward Lyle. Toward Hayley.

Just three of us now. Me, Lyle, and Hayley. His eyes are dilated, giant black depths of pain. "You go," he says "I can't hurt no dog."

I want more than anything to disappear into the crowd of police, to take off the costume, to wash off the sweat and the fear and be just Emma again. I want to take a hot shower, curl up on my couch with Rufus's head in my lap, and cradle a mug of cinnamon tea. I want it so badly I can taste the cinnamon. The police can take him down. They have guns. What do I have?

I hear a moan. Hayley. "When the whimper of welcome is stilled (how still!)." I can't let that whimper go still. I stroke Hayley's arm, rubbing the arm around her as well.

Lyle's lip shakes. "Go. You get down now."

Tears merge with sweat and the runoff from my nose, all hidden by Chester's grinning head.

I lean in so Hayley can pat Chester's head. Then I hold out my arms. Give me Hayley. Come on. Give her to me.

Lyle's mouth opens, closes, then opens again. "I miss Ranger so much."

I hold my arms stiff against a gust of wind. I know that tear at the heart. I'd be his Ranger, just for a moment.

He swings his arm open, and I grab Hayley into a furry embrace. Shots fire and Lyle falls. The pain in his eyes flickers and vanishes. No more twitching. I can't help crying even harder.

Through strands of Hayley's hair, I watch police run onto the stage and surround the euthanized man. An officer reaches for Hayley, but she clutches my neck, her body a tug of war rope. I lift each little finger gently, kissing them with Chester's mouth, until I'm free of her.

I step toward the swarm around Lyle, aching to give him one last hug for Ranger, but the officers lift me off the stage. I almost resist, but I feel the grass through Chester's paws and I stagger with relief.

A crowd rushes toward me, straining against a thin line of police. I hear the words hero and brave, and I don't care.

My hands shake as I lift Chester's head off my shoulders, letting in the cool breeze to work on the tears and sweat. I nearly pass out from the ecstasy of it.

Brendan jumps up and down amid the surging crowd to get my attention, his grin confirming an unshaken faith in a painless world. For him, this is still a county park on a spectacular fall day. For me, it will never be a place of joy again.

"Emma! Emma!" He waves furiously.

I point a paw, the police let him through and he rushes to me.

"Emma, you were amazing!" He lets go of Rufus's leash.

I fall to my knees and Rufus jumps on me, his tongue scrubbing the sweat and tears from my nose, my eyes, my cheeks. His red body sinks into Chester's black fur and his tail thwacks my knees as I cry into his cheek.

He licks my neck as I say his name. "Rufus. Rufus." I kiss his notched ear.

He tears at my heart and it's wonderful. 🔫

A GRAVE MISTAKE

Rachel Amphlett

It was the sound of his panicked breathing that scared Ben the most.

A late autumn sun collapsed beneath a line of naked hornbeam and oak, its rays shrivelling against a pale grey sky that receded through an expanse of tangled branches.

The last tentacles of heat retreated from a dirt path, withered away under rotten ferns and bracken, then surrendered the woodland to a damp biting cold.

He tipped back his head and swore.

A blackbird scuttled out from under a buckthorn shrub then took flight, its brittle parting cry rebuking him for the disturbance.

Ahead, an algae-covered pond sat nestled within a grove of birch trees, taunting him.

It was their third meeting within the space of forty minutes.

The stench hadn't improved since their last parting, the rancid aroma from the stagnant water wafting on the breeze.

He placed his hands on his hips, and then turned his back on the fetid pool and took off down the next fork in the path, a renewed urgency in his stride.

This route was narrower, twisted, less used.

The boughs above his head crowded in as if curious to know who walked amongst them.

Hazel saplings poked and prodded at his padded black jacket that looked great, but allowed every cold tentacle of wind to wrap its way around his body as he pushed his way through the thickening undergrowth.

He began to hum under his breath, a tune from his college years to fight against the silence encroaching with every step.

His heart rate quickened at a gap in the trees, the promise of escape.

He hurried, stumbled forward, broke through the branches that barricaded his way.

Then stopped.

In the glade, under a natural arch of oak and ash and accompanied by a choir of flies, was a grave.

Fresh.

Scuff marks scratched the dirt around it, scraped and scoured to create a hole, then backfilled in a hurry.

Dead leaves covered the churned soil, a feeble attempt to hide the secrets beneath.

Ben swallowed.

Somewhere off to his left, a twigged cracked, the noise as loud as a shotgun as it echoed amongst the tree trunks.

He bolted for a narrow path leading off to the right that soon became clogged with saplings and tendrils of ivy.

Reaching a crossroads in the dirt, he spun around, hands clasped on top of his head, his gaze sweeping left and right.

The late afternoon sun had turned to twilight now, shadows deepening and crawling towards him from the gloom between the undergrowth.

Pausing to pull out his mobile phone, he held it aloft and snarled at the screen.

There was no signal here, no way to check his location or work out where he went wrong.

Ben's gaze fell to the path as he shoved the phone back in his pocket.

He froze.

Something had been dragged through here.

Something heavy.

He checked over his shoulder.

The scuff marks continued east, two parallel lines carving an uneven path.

Towards the grave.

His eyes followed the scuff marks as they disappeared into the distance, heading west.

Fear turned to desperation—maybe that was the way back to the park entrance.

Maybe that was the way out.

He set off, started humming again, a habit borne of nerves.

No birds accompanied him now; no far-off calls and whistles reached his ears.

Afraid to stop, afraid to register the silence that was so alien to him, Ben ploughed on, his pace quickening with every passing second.

He broke into a run, swiping his hands at the thin reed-like saplings, ducking under low branches.

Sweat beaded across his forehead, pooled between his shoulder blades as his lungs heaved from the exertion.

Ben blinked as the trees began to thin out and the path began to widen.

He could hear voices then.

Close, so close.

Just a little farther to go …

Ben stumbled into the clearing beside a sign for car parking, his boots sliding on the gravel surface as he came to a halt and raised his hand to shield his eyes from blinding headlights.

Two uniformed police officers turned to face him.

The younger of the two officers rested a hand against his radio as it emitted a squawk, and called out.

'Is this your vehicle?'

Ben ran his hand through his hair, plucked out an errant twig that had caught in his fringe and gulped a lungful of air, his heart hammering.

'Is there a problem?'

The older officer circled the car, the beam from his flashlight arcing over the windscreen, the radiator grille, the license plate splashed with mud.

The younger officer—McLaren, according to the stripe opposite his badge—repeated his question.

'Is this your vehicle?'

'It is. Is the park closed? I got lost.'

Both men took a step back as he put his hand in his pocket, fingers twitching near their weapons.

'Hands where we can see them, sir.' The other one, Thomas, barked the words.

'It's just my keys.' He jangled them, dangling them from his forefinger and thumb. 'I need to get back—my wife will be wondering where I am.'

Their expressions changed then, a flash of something flitting across McLaren's features.

'Can you open the trunk, sir?'

Ben fumbled the keys on his first attempt, then aimed the fob at the car and blinked as the indicator lights flashed.

Thomas moved to his side as he reached out for the lid, a hand outstretched. 'Slowly.'

A reluctant sigh escaped Ben as he opened the trunk and McLaren stepped forward.

His flashlight swung over the bloodied blanket, the discarded shoe, the mobile phone with its cracked screen.

All hers.

All the things he planned to dispose of once he finished digging the grave.

'What have you done with your wife, Ben? Where did you bury her?'

He choked out a laugh tinged with irony and regret.

'How the hell would I know? I told you, I got lost.'

ONLY THE DESPERATE COME HERE

Michael Mallory

His phone rang six times before Scott Turley located it. He still used a flip-top "geezer" phone even though he was not yet fifty. Aside from the cost factor of having a so-called "smart" phone, he had no interest in games, or selfies, or any of the other nonsense people these days did. All he needed was something to get and make calls.

He just wished he could locate the damned thing before the caller gave up.

Whoever it was had to be a stranger. Anyone who knew Turley knew better than to call after six in the evening, when he already had a load on.

What's more, whoever it was had to be desperate. Only the desperate came to him.

"Finally," he slurred upon spotting the phone in the covers of his bed. "A'turley Scott 'torney," he answered.

"Is this Scott Turley?" a voice asked.

"I just said it was." He drained the last of the Old Crow from the fifth.

"I need a lawyer," the voice said. "I killed a man."

Turley stayed silent for a second, and then said, "Repeat that."

"I said I killed a man. I need a lawyer."

"Are you calling from a p'lice station?"

"No. I haven't been arrested, but I'm afraid I will be."

"Okay, look, why don't you come to my office tomorrow. You know where it is?"

"Yes. Thank you."

"'Leven o'clock."

"I'll be early."

"You'll be alone, then, 'cause I get in at 'leven o'clock. What the hell's your name, anyway?"

"Carl Bone the third."

"The son of the city councilman?"

"That's right."

He hadn't had a lot of dealings with Councilman Carl Bone, Jr., but he knew all the scuttlebutt. Springfield wasn't so big and deep that it could support an ocean of secrets. Junior Bone had inherited a thriving car dealership from his father but the word on the street was that his business dealings were shady. It was said he owned a chop shop in one of the nearby smaller towns which serviced his used car division.

Then again, you couldn't believe every bit of gossip you heard.

"You still there, Mr. Turley?" Bone the third asked.

"Where else would I be? 'Leven o'clock tomorrow morning. See ya."

He cut off the call.

If this kid was a Bone, there would be money in the case. He tore open a brand new fifth of Crow and took a long pull directly from the bottle to celebrate his good fortune.

Scott Turley's office was on the street level of an old Wilson-era hotel that housed a handful of seniors and indigents. It was on a one-time commercial hot spot that was now on its knees begging for redevelopment. Some hotshot urban developer had been threatening to buy the place and evict all the tenants, but various advocacy groups in the city had managed to forestall that. Turley was fighting it in court too, so as not to lose the best rent-controlled office space in the city.

That was important because he figured clients would not want to consult with him at his residence—a room at the YMCA.

The next morning when Turley arrived, he saw a car was parked in front of his building. Figuring it was his client—early, as promised—he walked past.

Less than a minute after he'd unlocked his door and switched on the lights, Carl Bone III knocked on the door jamb. He was tall, blond, well-dressed, and still had the stink of college about him. Bone stepped up and introduced himself, after which Turley directed him to a plastic chair on the other side of his aging desk.

"I'd offer you coffee but I haven't made it yet," the attorney said.

"That's okay, I don't drink coffee."

"All right, Mr. Bone, tell me about your problem," he said.

It wasn't so much a sad tale as a stupid one. Bone worked for the city in the procurement office, thanks to his father's influence, but moonlighted in a bar at the edge of town at night, for extra cash. Three nights ago, a drunken former college classmate came in itching to start a fight. The bouncer threw the guy out, which seemed like the end of the problem. But after closing, Bone found the guy waiting for him in an alley beside the bar. The fight was over a girl they'd both dated, and it ended only when Bone picked up an empty bottle in the alley and broke it over his rival's head.

"He fell down and I ran away," Bone finished. "The next day his body was found there."

"Does *he* have a name?" Turley asked.

"Mark Kessler."

Turley's desk chair gave a rusty scream as he leaned forward. "This is very important," he said. "Do you know for a fact that Mark Kessler was dead when you left?"

"No. But I'm afraid someone else might have seen me running away from the alley."

"That time of night?"

"The bar had only just closed. A lot of times there are still people hanging around."

"All right. What happened to the bottle?"

"You mean the one I broke over his head?"

No, moron, the one the genie came out of! Turley thought, but held his tongue. "That's the one I mean, yes," he finally said.

"It was broken."

"I got that. But I assume you held onto the neck to swing it. Did you simply drop the neck after it broke?"

"Oh, I ... I guess I tossed it in the dumpster as I ran away. Was that a mistake?"

"No, it's a good thing. Maybe the police won't find it."

"But what if they do?" Bone asked.

The chair screamed again as Turley leaned back. "What we have here is possible manslaughter, though the fact that you don't know if Kessler was actually dead when you fled the scene leaves a pretty sizeable footprint for reasonable doubt."

Part of him wanted to tell the young idiot to go to the police and explain what happened, and maybe even swear that the victim was still alive when he ran out. But while confession might be good for the soul, it was terrible for billable legal fees.

"If I take this case, I'll need a five-thousand-dollar retainer," he told the kid. "In cash."

"Ouch."

"Sorry, but that's the way the law business works. You can go to someone else if you want, but based on what you've told me so far, I'm not sure who'd take you on as a client."

"I know. That's why I'm here. Okay, I can get the money."

"Good. And from this moment on you talk to no one but me about this. That includes the police if they come around. From now on I do all the talking. You got that?"

Charles Bone III nodded.

"Good. I am curious about something, though. You said you came here because you knew I'd take on the case, despite the fact that you already admitted to me your guilt. Who tipped you off? Your father?"

"Good god, no," Bone said. "He doesn't know about this at all. If he did, he'd kill me himself. It was someone else who works at the bar, Pedro Alvarez. He said you got him off on a burglary charge a couple years ago."

"Oh, Pedro Alvarez," Turley said, having no recollection of ever handling a client by the name. But he rarely remembered old clients. Once the bill was paid, they were nothing more than a piece of paper in a file. "Okay, you get me that retainer, and I'll see what I can do for you."

Scott Turley spent the next day looking for any information about the victim. At the library he combed through the last weeks' worth of newspapers, finding a story about the murder in the Tuesday edition. Twenty-four-year-old Mark Kessler lived in the city but had no known occupation. Then Turley read something that changed everything: while the police had noticed an abrasion on the dead man's head, that wasn't what killed him.

What caused Kessler's heart to cease beating was the bullet that went straight into it.

The Bone kid didn't say anything about carrying a gun, which meant someone else had to have killed Kessler. That was good … at least for his client.

Going into the bathroom of the library, Turley pulled out his cell and dialed a number. Sergeant Wes Corson answered.

"Hi, Wes, it's Scott Turley."

After a long sigh, the police sergeant said, "What do you want now?"

"Just a little favor."

"I thought our statute of limitations had run out."

"Oh, that's no way to talk to an old friend." *Particularly one who saved your ass, your career, and your pension by giving you an alibi for that hit-and-run incident.* "What I want is very simple. I want to know whether you guys have a suspect for the shooting of that kid the other night, Kessler."

"If we don't, do you want to confess?"

"Hardee har."

"The Kessler killing isn't my case."

"But you could find out, right? Just ask a couple questions, do a quick hit ... and run?"

After another sigh, Corson said, "Yeah," and hung up.

Turley was sitting in a bar near the library building an hour later when the policeman called back.

"The bouncer was pulled in for questioning and he confirmed that there was some kind of altercation between Kessler and the bartender," Corson said. "He professed not to know anything about the murder. He hasn't risen to the level of suspect yet."

"Has anyone else?"

"I haven't heard about anyone else. The tecs on the case are concentrating on finding the gun."

"All right. Thanks, Wes. You're a real prince."

"Sure." The policeman hung up.

Armed with that information, Turley called the number Bone had given him, but was forced to leave a message.

By four the kid had not called him back, and Turley decided to knock off early. He was nearly out the door when the kid appeared, holding a book.

"I thought I'd come in person," Bone said, handing him an envelope.

Opening it, Turley saw that it was filled with c-notes. "I'm glad you did," he said. "Come on in."

"It looks like you were about to leave."

"I was, but every afternoon is a fluid situation." Sticking the envelope in his breast pocket, he took his seat behind the desk. "You don't read the papers, do you?" he asked Bone.

"No, why?"

"If you did, you'd know Kessler wasn't killed from a blow to the head. He was shot."

"With a gun?"

"That's generally the best way to do it. So unless you were carrying a gun, you didn't kill him. Were you carrying a gun?"

"I don't own a gun. Am I in the clear now? Did I just pay you five-thousand dollars for nothing?"

"Hardly. I cannot honestly declare that you're home free yet. I pulled some strings to find out that the police brought in the bouncer from your bar for questioning. What, if anything, he told them about you I have no way of knowing. So for the time being, you're still stuck with me."

Something struck Turley then.

"If you don't read the papers," he asked, "how'd you even learn that Kessler was dead?"

"Well, it was all over the bar the next night."

"That makes sense." Looking at the book Bone was holding, Turley asked, "What's that you've got there?"

"It's my college yearbook. Mark went to the same college. He was a sophomore while I was a senior. I put a yellow sticky on the page with his picture. Since this is the only piece of evidence that connects the two of us prior to the fight, I thought you might want to see it."

Maybe the kid isn't as dumb as he seems, Turley thought, taking the book.

"What should I do now?" Bone asked.

"Like I said, I have no idea if the police are going to show up to talk to you or not. If they do, don't say anything. Call me, no matter what time it is."

After Bone was gone Turley closed up the office and headed for the local convenience store for a couple bottles before going back to his room at the Y.

He was flagged down at the desk of the Y by the clerk, who told him he had a package.

"From who?" Turley asked, hoping his most recent ex-wife hadn't finally found him.

The clerk shrugged and handed over the small, plainly wrapped box which bore only his address. "Came special delivery," he said.

Taking it, Turley headed up to his room. After stashing the balance of the five grand (minus the cost of the booze) in the top drawer of his dresser, he tore open a bottle of Old Crow and the package, in that order.

Wrapped in tissue inside, he found the last thing he expected: a .44 caliber handgun and a few credit cards.

"What the hell is this?" he demanded of the cardboard container, which didn't answer.

Opening the gun, he saw four bullets in the chamber. Were they blanks? Shaking them out into his hand proved they were not.

His stomach sank even deeper when he examined the credit cards: each one was issued to Marcus L. Kessler.

"What the hell's going on here?" he shouted.

Almost as if to answer, his room phone rang. Turley picked it up.

"This is Alben down at the desk," the voice at the other end said. "I wanted to make sure you were in your room."

"Where the hell else would I be?"

The line cut off.

Turley was still puzzling over the gun and the credit cards when he heard people approaching in the hallway, followed by a pounding on his door. "Police, open up," a voice called.

"Shit!" he hollered, forcing the bullets back into the chamber and hiding it, and the cards, under his mattress.

More pounding came, and this time Turley called back, "Hold your horses, I'm coming."

Opening the door, he saw two policemen and the desk clerk standing in the hall, backed by four more tenants who were wondering what the hell was going on. "Can we come in, sir?" one of the cops asked.

"Why?"

"We can do this the easy way or the hard way."

"Or you can turn around and leave."

"Sir, we just need a few words with you."

"Which you can state right where you are. If you want to set foot inside this room, though, you'd better get a warrant."

"Why, what are you hiding?"

"I'm not hiding anything. I'm displaying my rights."

Now the other officer spoke. "Whatever it is you are hiding; it must be small. There's not a lot of room here."

"Hey, Ben, see that?" the first cop said. "The bedding is pushed in in the middle, like something's there. A gun, maybe?"

"Do you own a gun, sir?"

"No, I ... I ... ask him!" Turley pointed at the clerk. "He's the one who gave me the package with the goddamn pistol. Ask him where he got it?"

"I think you should come with us, sir," Officer Ben said.

Instead, Turley slammed the door in their faces. Rushing back to the bed, he pulled out the gun and the cards, and stuffed them back in the box. Then he tried to figure out how to get rid of it. Tossing it outside was the best option he could think of.

Turley opened the room's tiny window and held the box out, then dropped it ... a second before noticing the policeman below waiting patiently to catch it.

This was not the first time Scott Turley found himself in a holding cell, but it was by far for the most serious charges.

During questioning, he learned that the police had come to the Y as a result of an anonymous phone tip by someone who claimed to have seen Turley shoot Mark Kessler in the alley. The yearbook, with the picture of Kessler marked, and the five thousand in cash found in his room strongly implied it was a hit for hire.

Turley opted to defend himself in the arraignment hearing, but was hard pressed to come up with any kind of defense except to say that he had been framed by person or persons unknown. His professionalism in court was further compromised by recurring bouts of the DTs. When confronted with the evidence against him—the ballistics tests proving that the bullets in the gun, which he had attempted to get rid of, matched the slug in Kessler's body; as well as the yearbook, credit cards, and money that had been similarly found in his room—the DA's office began badgering Turley to take a plea deal.

"This is such a slam-dunk, we don't want to waste taxpayer money on a trial," assistant DA Monica Brundage told him. "We even have the sworn statement of police sergeant Wesley Corson that you called him up trying to find out whether you were on the suspect list or not."

"That's not why I called him!" Turley insisted. "I called him on behalf of a client. I told you that. Carl Bone the third. He's the real killer."

"The same Carl Bone the third who proved he was not even in the city the night of the murder?"

"He was! He was working at the bar!"

"Not according to the bouncer," Brundage said.

Turley's mind was swirling as violently as his hands were shaking.

"Look," he said, "whatever you think of me, I'm still a member of the legal profession. I know how things work! You wouldn't be offering me a plea if you were so sure you had a case. You only offer pleas when you think there's a good chance you're going to lose."

She leaned forward over the table and smiled. Young and dark-haired, she reminded Turley too much of his second wife.

"I'm offering the plea because even though we've got you dead-to-rights for the murder, we don't believe it was your idea," ADA Brundage said. "You tell us who hired you and the death penalty is automatically off the table, and we might even be able to reduce the charges."

"But I didn't …!"

Turley stopped talking then.

"All right, Mr. Turley. If you really want to take your chance in court, representing yourself, with the death penalty back on the table, I guess I'm wasting my time."

She got up to leave.

"It was the father," Turley said. "Carl Bone, Jr. He hired me."

"*Councilman Bone* is the man who hired you?" she cried. Then she laughed, long and loud. "You're going to have to do a *lot* better than that. See you in court, Mr. Turley."

"This is the last time, you understand me?" Carl Bone Jr. told his son on the day of Scott Turley's sentencing. "You kill someone else in a fight, you get out of it yourself, including finding your own fall guy."

"I get it, I get it," Carl III replied. "And I appreciate what you did for me."

His father leveled a finger at him and gave him one of *those* glares. "I mean it, *Trey*. The *last* time. Just paying off the staff of your damn bar to lie about your presence there cost me a hundred-thousand."

"But you've got your building."

"True enough. I guess it all evens out in the end."

Councilman Carl Bone, Jr., smiled, knowing that the last legal thorn preventing him from evicting all that dead weight from his newly-acquired residential hotel had effectively been neutralized … and through the death penalty yet! "When will the little people of this city learn not to screw with me?" he asked.

"Never, Dad," his son dutifully replied. 🖝

A LITTLE HOUSECLEANING

David Bart

His last partner would've said Wade was being haunted by the dead farmer lying there on the kitchen floor; like his ghost was groaning and moaning.

Wade shook his head, chuckling. Hell, all these old farmhouses across the Nebraska flatlands creak and groan. "Ain't some silly damn ghost," he said.

He glanced at his reflection in the night-blackened kitchen window. "Are you talkin' to me?"

Classic De Niro.

Anyway, if there were ghosts, he'd have seen them by now; he'd snatched the life out of enough people during his forty-six years, surely they'd have bitched to him long before now.

Wade thumbed his lighter, a tiny orange flame appearing in the dark window pane—lit the butt and took a sustained drag; the searing in his chest reminded him of the scalding shame he'd felt after his first foster mother had caught him smoking. "*Stupid little bastard, stealing my butts.*" Smacked his six-year-old head—*stars bursting*—odor of cheap tequila and unwashed hair.

He'd had four more "moms" since then. Most okay, but that one had been a mean-spirited harpy.

Course, smoking *was* bad for you ... but then so was refusing Wade Calvert something, as the old farmer would've learned if he'd survived. You don't refuse Wade entry, particularly when it's threatening rain. A prison librarian and a few partners in crime had all learned a simple lesson: *you don't refuse Wade Calvert anything.*

"Whatta you want, boy?" the old farmer had growled earlier, leathery face pinched into the dour look of a man who judged the world harshly.

Wade savored the smell of something hot and spicy bubbling on the stove, telling the old man, "A little hospitality, dude."

The irascible farmer had hissed, "Get off my place or I'll call the cops." Started to swing the door closed, but Wade reared back, kicked the solid wood entry door into the old man's head, dropping him like a sledgehammered steer onto the slaughterhouse killing floor.

And then he'd just stood very still, listening ... a faint sound beyond the kitchen, then quiet. Except for the freshening wind.

The oozing blood at his feet reminded him of a meatpacking outfit in Omaha that he'd quit after just a couple hours, some burly butcher writhing on the floor, Wade's boning knife jutting from the guy's leg, a femoral artery spouting bright red blood like a festive fountain. The big dufus hadn't liked being called a "clod-pated bovine" and had shoved Wade into the trimming table, the impact dumping hunks of meat onto the floor.

You don't shove Wade.

You don't refuse Wade.

You don't ...

... he glanced around the kitchen ... he'd blanked out for a bit, this wasn't an Omaha slaughterhouse. Wade stared at the blood pooling around the farmer's head, glossy red against the pea-green linoleum.

The old man groaned and Wade blinked a few more times ... why didn't he ever feel sympathy or regret after assaulting someone?

He hopped over the body and playfully sniffed at steam rising off the pot on the stove. "What's a cookin'?"

Course, he knew. The chili they served once a week in the slam smelled like that, the tub-a-guts cook claiming he spit in Wade's bowl. "For added flavor, convict."

A battered red coffee mug sat on the countertop. He examined it curiously, a chip out of the rim as white as a busted tooth. Wade ladled the bubbling red chili from pot to bowl using the battered mug. "Best be *con carne*," he said, stepping over the blood and sitting at the table.

And then he spit in the bowl. For added flavor.

Miriam was huddled in an empty cow stall, her back against moldy wood planks, armfuls of fragrant hay pulled around her to keep in body heat. She had, thankfully, escaped through the summer kitchen at the house, sloshing through chill puddles in the lawn, arthritic knees screaming at her.

Shivering in the stall it was hard to ignore the itchiness and an overpowering urge to sneeze. A single question repeated in her brain: Where had he come from?

Wade stubbed his cigarette on the table top, red sparks reminding him of—

Damn, he *hated* fireworks, all those oohs and aahs of kids and their normal families. He bet those pampered little shits had never been dragged by the hair past an ice cream stand at the summer fair, chocolaty torture of hot fudge taunting them.

He'd had plenty of sundaes as an adult though, sometimes eating one while a partner scooped out the till, the dumbass thinking Wade would share their meager take.

The latest of his double-crosses had been stiffing ol' Carl out of the money they'd boosted from Bucks a' Plenty, a tawdry check-cashing shop in Kearney ... buried the crook in a riverside copse of green willow outside of town, the easterly wind carrying the constant whine of traffic from I-80. It'd been hard going, the sandy soil backfilling the grave as he dug.

He'd stood there afterwards, river breeze cooling his face, Sandhill Cranes wading in the shallow Platte, the dying sun alchemizing river water into molten copper. The stilted gait of the cranes and their odd vocalizations were annoying at first, but soon felt strangely soothing ... he couldn't say why. Stupid birds.

Then the blowout on an eerily familiar blacktop road ...

They'd jacked the van from a friendly salesman outside a roadside bar, Wade giving the idiot the kind of head blow from which you don't fully recover ... did the same for Carl, buried him in the willows, then got a flat, which is when he'd discovered the van carried a ruined spare. Apparently, the salesman believed nothing bad could happen to him.

Ultimately Wade found himself alone, dusk gathering, a chill wind promising an imminent storm, confirmed by the blackening sky to the west. Wade gazed across the sea of dry, windblown corn, the dry stalks rattling like brittle bones. The first fat drops got him moving toward the old farmhouse, white clapboard siding ghostly pale in the deepening gloom.

Rachel peered over the twin beams tunneling through the darkness like ... *Goddamned promises.*

It'd been a hard day but she kept on tooling west along I-80. The sky had darkened well before dusk ... all she needed now was a friggin' tornado to blow her to the Emerald City.

No wait, wasn't it too late in the season? Had climate change screwed that up too? God, she'd had enough violence in her life. But thankful that she still looked good, had a great body, minimal wrinkles. Single fathers picking up their kids at the day care had for some time taken notice of her: dinner invitations, yearning looks.

Men. Can't live with them, cold sheets without them.

Course, the worst one had been gone a few years, out of her life. Took a good portion of the pain with him. But not all.

And now here she was, rolling backwards in time down this rough interstate, every cell in her body telling her to turn around and go back to her little apartment in Lincoln, sparsely furnished but replete with cats.

Damn it. She'd had enough of that desolate country life, those backward people.

Rachel flicked on the turn signal for the next exit ... turned it back off and sped by the exit, smacking the steering wheel as she continued on down the road.

Goddamned promises.

While eating all the chili Wade had also wolfed down some stale saltines and mold-veined cheddar—*not that bad, had worse in the slam.*

The old man groaned from the kitchen floor, spindly legs jerking in a running motion like a dreaming dog ... a final twitch and then dead still.

"You should've been nicer," Wade said, not expecting a response, though irritated when he didn't get one. Prodded the corpse with his foot. "See what being rude got you."

He sat there for an hour, only distantly aware of the ticking clock, oblivious to how much time had passed ... suddenly knelt down, rummaging to find only three twenties and six singles in the old man's worn wallet—*what in hell can you buy with that?* And where're the truck keys—there was a muddy black Ford F-150 in the barn. Locked.

Wade stuffed the dead presidents into his pocket with an anger cultivated by long use—*and here's an image of the old farmer shuffling out every goddamned morning after grumbling into his Quaker Oats, pissed at the sun for rising, tending some scrawny chickens, flicking meager bits of grain as he trudged toward the sad patch of weed-infested dirt he called a garden. High point of late summer for the old man would've been ripping a fat tomato off its vine, chomping down, the acidic juice dripping off his grizzled chin like watery blood.*

Wade gazed disinterestedly at the farmer's body on the floor. Yawned. Full tummy, but in the morning he'd scarf up those brown-shell eggs in the old guy's antiquated fridge before he hit the road. Have to cook 'em himself—scrambled, with a sprinkle of cayenne from the little bottle on the counter. It's what made the chili hot and spicy.

At the bottom of the stairs he twisted the button on the antiquated light switch—frowned at a sense of déjà vu—the dangling bare bulb offered little more than twilight in the steep stairway, cobwebs brushing his face as he ascended. The stale air was redolent with faint odors he couldn't identify, though were somehow dreamingly familiar.

At the top of the narrow stairs Wade paused, a bit winded. Christ, must've taken the old man an hour to get up to bed every night.

He studiously ignored the rattling sound outside the window; the pale face he'd just glimpsed must've been a hallucination. Shrinks told him they'd appear to him more and more as his sanity degraded. Course, psychiatrists were crazier than their patients; two of his prison shrinks had been certifiable, one of them staring at the ceiling and humming over steepled fingers while Wade emptied his guts.

The rattling sound stopped and he relaxed a bit, saying aloud, "It's the second floor, idjit, nobody could be out there, no such thing as ghosts."

He got up and looked down to the dark lawn. Nothing. Looked out toward the interstate and wondered at the golden stream of moving lights; folks traveling, visiting, moving to another life; with their own stories, problems.

His third foster dad, a guy who'd sold drugs in Omaha, had used him as a delivery kid. The nasty bastard could sure make his tiny wife *fly;* sailed her across the kitchen like a Frisbee.

But one day, confronted by a big-for-his-age Wade, he'd said, "I'll do what I want with *my* wife, so hit the bricks ya little bastard!"

Amazing the damage you can do to a guy's head with a four-hole toaster; left plugged in while you're pounding makes a lot of sparks.

She felt more alone than ever. Miriam was shivering, upper plate chattering. What had she been thinking? Peeking in an upstairs window, teetering on a ladder in a stormy wind. *Foolish old woman. Might've broke your neck.*

Aloud, she said to her internal voice, "Just wanted to make sure it was him."

Miriam opened the barn door a crack, slipped back inside without a sound, her nose already twitching at the sneezy odor of hay.

"Oh, my God—Frank?"

Wade squinted, looking away from the harsh morning sunlight streaming through the smudged upstairs windows—no face looking in this morning. He sat up in bed, listening to … what?

From downstairs. A woman's voice. Must've been what had awakened him. He crept down the stairs barefoot, amazed at his luck when he looked into the kitchen.

She was kneeling beside the dead chili maker, her shoulders convulsing like someone silently laughing. Looked disheveled, like she'd been driving all night.

"Hey, darlin', likes me some eggs, pronto," he said, scratching himself.

She rose, whirling around, eyes wide, frightened—ultra-curvy body like you see working a stripper's pole.

"What are you doing here?" she croaked.

"Just get me my eggs, woman."

She frowned, confused.

And then bolted—

Prison-quick he slammed his fist into her jaw and she crumpled to the floor. His hand stung, but he dragged her unconscious body to the living room couch and began unbuckling his belt. There's all kinds of hunger.

The old woman was hunched over, trying to catch her breath, the direct sunlight brightening her face, though her eyes were opaque like milky-blue marbles. Miriam had needed cataract surgery for some time, but Frank wouldn't pay or let her use Medicare.

"You okay?" the young woman asked, pausing with one foot on top of the shovel blade, breathing deeply. "Miriam, I can't believe you climbed a ladder to look in that bedroom window."

The old woman chuckled. "You mean 'cause I'm 'old as dirt'?" Nodded at the pile of black soil.

They'd dumped an unconscious Wade into the hole, the young woman now tossing a bucket of icy well water into his face, wholly indifferent to his discomfort, just as she'd learned to silently suffer his beatings over the years.

Wade blinked, eyes stinging. Took a few beats to get his bearings … on either side of him black dirt walls rose to a rectangle of hopeful blue sky—but why was his face *wet*? Two dark forms stood at the rim, the sun behind them. On his face he felt the soft whisper of a breeze drifting down to him, like a victim's last breath.

He was screwed, no question; but he figured what the hell, give it a shot anyway: "Mom? Wife? We gotta stop meeting like this."

Rachel said, "I'm glad you knocked him out before he could … you know."

His ex thanking her sorta-mother-in-law.

Wade chuckled. "Don't hold that against me, they tell me I'm not right in the head."

The old woman's voice was as calming as ever. "Wade, I told you a thousand times, there's no excuse for rude behavior. Now it's left to us to clean up some *man's* mess, as women been doing for centuries."

Wade probed his cheek with his tongue. Might as well give it one final try. "When you weren't at the house, I guess I figured you'd passed away. Made me kinda sad," he said to Miriam.

Shovels began slicing through wet dirt, compacted clods pummeling him as he struggled against the bonds. Guess Miriam wasn't the sentimental type.

He knew he was bonkers, didn't need a shrink to tell him that; but he was sane enough to know that when it's over, it's over. His squirming made him aware of a corpse beneath him. The grave was for both him and Frank, his last foster father. And latest victim.

"Why do you suppose he came back here?" Rachel said as they made their way back to the farmhouse, squawking white hens fluttering out of the way, one taking refuge under a red wheelbarrow that was still dripping from last night's storm.

The old woman shrugged, not really wanting to talk about it ... she had tried to be a surrogate mother to a young Wade, thought of him as her own son. "Maybe he made a promise to himself, like the one you made to me to visit on my birthday."

The younger woman just shook her head in wonder. "So, what, we tell the police Frank went to Omaha two weeks ago to buy cattle, insisted on taking cash, thought he could bargain better?"

"The whole county knows about the benders Frank went on, cops will figure he got rolled for the money outside a bar, dumped in the Missouri."

"But why not tell the truth, Miriam, that Wade murdered Frank and then we got the better of him?"

"Told you, they'll think *we* were in on Frank's murder, me being the killer's foster-mother, beneficiary of Frank's insurance, and you being Wade's ex-wife. We're women who've been abused by both of them."

"What about his truck, wouldn't he have taken it? Omaha isn't all that far."

Miriam sighed. "Like I said, he took the bus, afraid to drive on the interstate— mostly elderly people on buses, wouldn't be remembered amongst all the old farmers who ride. Anyway, why would they check?"

The young woman stepped up onto the porch, reached down to help Miriam navigate the treacherous steps Frank had refused to repair year after year. He'd buy lumber and new tools for working on his stupid deer blind, but no way he'd do what a mere woman told him to do.

Wade's foster mother leaned forward to peer at the front door's bloody edge. "I need to clean that before I call the cops to give my missing person report."

Wade's ex-wife said, "I'll do it," went and got the cleaning supplies. She was done in ten minutes, then cleaned up the congealed blood from the kitchen floor, which took longer; started with a spatula to scrape up the thick part, then used paper towels and bleach.

Miriam said, "How 'bout a nice omelet?" Rubbed her hands together as she started toward the fridge for the brown-shell eggs and the last tomato of the season.

"You can get the cataract surgery now, watch your birds again," Rachel said.

The foster mother stopped, squinted at a nearby window where once she'd had a bird feeder. *Is that glass dirty? Or is it just my foggy eyes?* She remembered how her own grandmother used to say: "A house isn't clean until the windows sparkle." A sweet woman who wouldn't hurt a fly, though it was rumored she'd killed her husband. For country women, even in the Twenty-First century, it was an accepted remedy for unrelenting abuse.

There was a tongue-in-cheek code, whispered as they huddled over busy hands in quilting circles: *she must've done a little housecleaning.*

Miriam clapped her hands, suddenly animated. "I'll put cayenne in the eggs—in a kind of homage to Frank and Wade. Boys liked it hot and spicy."

She turned to the counter, deftly cracked two eggs against each other over a crockery mixing bowl, not even a fragment of shell falling into the bowl—cracked the remaining egg on the rim of the bowl, making a dull ringing sound ... her face reddened, embarrassed that there were only three eggs. Not a proper omelet for two people hungry from hard work.

Course, the plump tomato would stretch the eggs and she could blend in chopped green onion tops; buttered sourdough toast, fresh-brewed coffee. It'd be fine.

Miriam nodded to herself as she beat the eggs. *So nice of Rachel to remember my birthday.*

Rachel leaned against the counter, smiling warmly at an old woman busy with her labors. The lives we live, she thought.

Miriam was standing straighter than she had in years; shoulders back, legs straight, softly humming a frontier ballad about putting things right. 🔫

A NUMBERS GAME

A You-Solve-It by Bruce Harris

Winter ball. January. An aging, worried group of Yankees infielders find themselves uncharacteristically in Puerto Rico, each player attempting to remain relevant. In less than two months, spring training for the Yankees and several other teams will begin in Florida.

As a child, Rey Acosta wondered what it would be like inside a major league locker room; as a player, not as a homicide detective. Rookie phenom Benny Tasby lay at an awkward angle, dead. His head bludgeoned with a baseball bat. His buff- and blue-colored Gallaudet University Bison t-shirt and yellow shorts were covered with blood.

"By the looks of it," said Medical Examiner Luis Coa, "He saw the blow coming. He tried to ward it off," pointing to a nasty purplish bruise on Tasby's left forearm. "He saw his killer."

In addition to Acosta, Coa, and the dead man, four veteran Yankees infielders stood in a semi circle. Third baseman Roy Sinclair, number 22, wore pressed jeans and an open collared starched white shirt. Shortstop, number 6 Wally Hermann rocked a designer Hawaiian print shirt and a matching, made-to-order Hawaiian print Yankees cap. The hat was turned around the same way catchers wear their caps during a game. The second baseman, number 3 Pete Pellicone was shirtless. His skin, already tanned by the tropical sun was tattoo covered. He wore bicycle shorts and sandals. Lastly, first baseman Cecil Brown, number 9, stoically stood in a neon pink pinstripe suit that wasn't purchased off any store rack. Acosta thought Brown appeared ready to step into Harlem's Cotton Club in its heyday. The tall, lanky first baseman noticed Acosta's gaze.

"I'm old school," Brown said. "To a point." His grin revealed straight white teeth. "Before you ask, detective, the skipper asked the five of us to stay a little late and to discuss among ourselves a few different defensive shift alignments. No one expected anything like this," Brown added, pointing to the dead Tasby.

"I wonder," Detective Acosta replied. He looked over the group. "I read the sports pages and blogs and listen to the talk shows. It's no secret that there was a good chance

Benny Tasby would be replacing one of you on the roster. He is … was … versatile and talented enough to play any infield position.”

“That’s a joke,” Sinclair said.

“Not really,” shortstop Hermann chimed in. “The Orioles … the lowly Orioles need a third baseman. It might have been more than just rumors that ownership was getting ready to ship your ass off to Baltimore and replace you with Tasby.”

Sinclair raised his middle finger.

“Nonsense,” second sacker Pellicone said. “We’re athletes, professionals. We welcome the competition. It brings out the best in us. That’s why we are all in Puerto Rico busting our tails instead of our homes.”

“Well, one of us killed Tasby,” Brown declared. He paused, and then continued sarcastically, “One of us professionals didn’t welcome the threat to his livelihood.” He took a breath. “Anyway, I’m in the clear.”

“How’s that?” Acosta asked.

“Look at Tasby’s statistics, detective. He spent no time in the minor leagues. He’s played what … a total of 20 college games at first base? He committed half-dozen errors. He wasn’t replacing me. I know how to catch a ball at first base. You’d best concentrate your efforts on these three.”

“I’ll take the advice under consideration,” Acosta dismissively said.

“How are you going to figure this out, detective?” Hermann asked. “No one saw anything, the killer isn’t about to confess his sin, and Tasby isn’t talking.”

“On the contrary,” the medical examiner said, shocking everyone including Acosta.

Doctor Coa rolled Tasby’s body a few inches, revealing the deceased’s right arm previously hidden under his chest. Tasby’s hand did the talking. His index, middle, and ring fingers were raised and separated. The tip of his thumb touched his pinky tip.

“Three!” Curtis announced. “He’s indicating the number 3.”

All eyes turned toward Pellicone.

“You!” Brown said using his most accusatory voice. “You’re number 3. You killed him! I knew it was you all along.”

Pellicone’s skin turned white. “I didn’t do it! I swear!”

“Not so fast,” Acosta warned everyone. “Pellicone is correct. He didn’t do it.

… Solution in next month’s issue …

SOLUTION TO JULY'S YOU-SOLVE-IT

POISONED RELATIONSHIP BY LAIRD LONG

Daphne poisoned Mabel. She was the only one who had access to Mabel's cup of tea when the other ladies weren't looking—three were at the front window and one was in the kitchen. The teapot or cookies couldn't have been poisoned, otherwise all five women would've been affected.